SWIFT TO ITS CLOSE
BY SIMON TROY

"Inspector Smith senses unpleasant undercurrents when he visits his friend Doyle Wantage, famous composer and founder of the Salchurch Music Festival. The inspector watches and listens as inevitably submerged hostilities surface in death."

SWIFT TO ITS CLOSE

BY SIMON TROY

PERENNIAL LIBRARY
Harper & Row, Publishers
New York, Cambridge, Philadelphia, San Francisco
London, Mexico City, São Paulo, Sydney

First PERENNIAL LIBRARY edition published 1981.

Designer: Susan Hull

ISBN: 0-06-080546-3

81 82 83 84 85 10 9 8 7 6 5 4 3 2 1

CONTENTS

SALCHURCH FESTIVAL CONCERTS

OPENING CONCERT OF THE SIXTH SEASON

Saturday September 10th 1966

New Western Symphony Orchestra

Conductor Hubert Tennier
Pianoforte, Colin Radwell

Overture, *Prometheus* . . . . Beethoven

Concerto for Piano and Orchestra, No. 24 in C Minor,
K 491 . . . . Mozart

Suite No. 2, *Daphnis and Chloe* . . . . Ravel

Symphony No. 1 in C Minor . . . . Brahms

ST. LUKE & ST. JAMES, SALCHURCH

Specification of the new organ built by N. P. Mander Ltd., designed by Ebor Maxton, Mus.Bac., F.R.C.O., in consultation with Noel Mander, Esq.

GREAT

Double Open Diapason	16'
Open Diapason I	8'
Open Diapason II	8'
Chimney Flute	8'
Principal	4'
Nason Flute	4'
12th	2⅔
15th	2'
Tierce	1⅗
Mixture	III
Fourniture	III
Contra Posaune	16'
Posaune	8'
Clarion	4'
Swell to Great	

POSITIVE

Stopt Diapason	8'
Principal	4'
Koppel Flute	4'
Nazard	2⅔
Spitz Flute	2'
Tierce	1⅗
Nineteenth	1⅓
Cymbal	III
Tremulent	

CHOIR (enclosed)

Contra Dulciana	16'
Lieblich Gedact	8'
Dulciana	8'
Wald Flute	4'
Salicet	4'
Lieblich Piccolo	2'
Corno di Bassetto	8'
Tuba	8'

Contra Posaune	} Great	16'
Posaune		8'
Clarion		4'

SWELL

Bourdon	16'
Gedact	8'
Salicional	8'
Vox Angelica	8'
Principal	4'
Lieblich Flute	4'
Fifteenth	2'
Mixture	III
Fagotto	16'
Cornopean	8'
Oboe	8'
Clarion	4'
Tremulant	
Choir/Pos to Great	

PEDAL

Contra Violone	32'
Open Wood	16'
Violone	16'
Bourdon	16'
Dulciana Bass	16'
Principal	8'
Bass Flute	8'
Fifteenth	4'
Choral Bass	4'
Piccolo	2
Mixture	IV
Double Ophicleide	32'
Ophicleide	16'
Fagotto	16'
Posaune	8'
Schalmei	4'
Swell to Pedal	
Great to Pedal	
Choir/Pos to Pedal	
Great & Pedal combs. coupled	

SWIFT TO ITS CLOSE

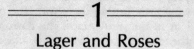

1

Lager and Roses

"I thought you were asleep," Doyle Wantage said from behind the canvas chair. "You haven't stirred an inch in the past half-hour."

Inspector Smith shook his grey head. "I never sleep during the day."

"And I never sleep at night. Every hour tolls for me, unless sheer exhaustion strikes me down. Something to do with one's metabolism."

The Inspector opened his eyes. "It's an occupational disease with you. At least you've something to show for it."

He was twelve miles from his usual beat. He might have been a hundred. There was nothing in this wide expanse of flat, marshy ground to remind him of his native coombes and coves. Nature plays such tricks. The Isle of Avalon lies under the Somerset hills, the lonely wastes of Braunton are enclosed by Exmoor foot-hills. Salchurch Marsh, where Smith was spending this summer afternoon, is a vast alluvial plain laid down by rivers that have now dwindled into creeks, a frag-ment of eastern England within sight of the Scillies.

It was June. Scent of hay and honeysuckle drifted along tree-shaded lanes, the nights were still under a crescent moon. Smith was to remember that day. It marked his first step towards an adventure that became odd and macabre as the summer wore away and developed in diabolic fashion, though its beginning seemed innocent enough, as beginnings often are.

A half-circular windbreak of trees sheltered the garden from what little breeze there was. The old house lay somnolent in the heat. Across the narrow lane at the foot of the tangled garden was a slow-moving creek. Beyond it stood the ruined mill which gave the place its name. Bargehouse Mill, a mile out of the village, linked with it by that lane and the watery ribbon which threaded the lush fields.

From the slight elevation of the garden, there was a panoramic view of those fields and the church tower and a grey-green expanse of sea beyond the low dunes. A brown-sailed boat seemed becalmed on the lower reaches of the creek. A woman walked slowly towards the house from Penrhuan way. Inspector Smith lit his pipe and let it go out again. It was pleasant to do nothing, nothing at all, merely to bake under the sun and contemplate a landscape which demanded so little attention.

Doyle Wantage hitched up his shapeless slacks. He was a tall, thin, stooping man with rusty hair and ferocious brows above mild brown eyes.

"And only man is vile!" he said. "Man and woman. Look at it. O peaceful England! Salchurch. Butter wouldn't melt in its mouth. Truly unspoilt. *On either side the river lie Long fields of barley and of rye, That clothe the earth and meet the sky* . . . What a bloody hornet's nest!"

Smith looked at him thoughtfully. It was a passing mood. Within five minutes he would be his own mellowed self again.

Doyle Wantage's father had been a Welshman from the Valleys who moved to Shilstone and kept a grocery shop across the street from Smith's police station. His mother came from Galway, hence his name. He was one of a large brood, a seventh child favoured by the

gods. At fifteen he was assistant organist of Shilstone
Old Church. Later he went to London and studied composition at the R.C.M.

That was the beginning of the Wantage legend. Since
those days he had grown shaggier in appearance, anar-
chical in musical matters, and less predictable in his
personal relationships. Smith was one of the few local
people who had kept in touch with him since his return
and the establishment of the Salchurch Festival.

"By the way, what have I to show for sleepless
nights?" he demanded.

"Eminence." Smith roused himself to the point of
striking another match. "With you, thinking is a cre-
ative occupation. So far as I'm concerned it's only retro-
spective. Or nostalgic, and that's even worse."

"I don't agree with you. Nostalgia is the most evoca-
tive emotion one can indulge in. I'm a nostalgic person.
I like this part of the country because I once lived for
three years in the Camargue. I look across these fields
and I can see wild bulls and flamingoes."

The Inspector nodded. "I envy you."

He was an inconspicuous man, more like a west-country farmer than a terror to evil-doers. His clothes were
slightly shabby, his hair slightly grey. Only his deep,
penetrating eyes gave any indication of his inward
strength. To be lulled by his burring voice and yet feel
the intense quality of those eyes—observing, considering, waiting—was an experience that had brought dis-
comfort to many a doubtful character in Shilstone and
Penrhuan.

"I shall never go back to the Camargue," Doyle Wantage said. "I had experiences there . . . We only become
truly nostalgic about things that are gone for ever. It's
the lost years that inspire our lieder. There are a few
songs of love and life triumphant. Cynical but true."

With his hands on Smith's chair, he watched the approaching figure. A young woman, walking slowly. In

that pale pastel landscape of corn and cloud and still water, she might have been a conventional figure, roughed in to give scale and a touch of humanity.

"Nobody I know," he said. "And there are very few people around here that I don't know."

She wore sandals, a short summer dress. Her hair was smooth and straight and pale, and touched her shoulders. She looked back towards the coast road, and forward towards Salchurch, as if uncertain which way to go. A footbridge over the creek seemed to interest her. She leaned against the rail, looking down at the water. Then with a long, thoughtful glance towards the house, she crossed the bridge and began to walk across the field.

"Definitely a stranger!" Doyle said. "That path looks as if it might be a short cut to Salchurch, but it ends at old Huxtable's drainage-ditch. And Huxtable keeps a bullock or two over there."

He hurried across the parched lawn and down the drive. The Inspector, watching with no great interest, saw the girl turn as Doyle called to her. There was a brief dialogue between them, inaudible at this distance, then they both came through the gate.

"It was a necessary warning. Huxtable should put up a board saying there's no way through. I suggested to this young lady that a long cool drink will help her along the lane. It's a mile to the village—three in this heat."

The Inspector conventionally lifted himself three inches from the canvas chair. "A happy thought!" he said.

"What would you like?" Doyle asked the girl. "Gin and something, lager? My name's Wantage, by the way. And this is Mr. Smith. He's a policeman. He once chased me for poaching salmon in the days of my innocence."

"Chased and caught you," Smith reminded him. The girl smiled. "Lager, please. It's very kind of you. . . . I'm Janice Teale."

"Nice name." Doyle peered at her, not inquisitively, but with great interest. "Very nice name. Sit down. No—here in the shade. It's damnably hot. Perhaps you like it this way?"

The Inspector smiled, remembering Doyle's voluble, defensive shyness of old. The girl didn't say whether she liked it or not, but he noticed the beads of perspiration on her upper lip, the dampness of her forehead.

"How far have you walked?" he asked, as Doyle Wantage lumbered off for the promised drinks.

"From Penrhuan."

She had a light, pleasant voice, with an attractively resonant timbre.

"That's quite a long way. I live just out of Penrhuan on the Shilstone road. On holiday?"

"Yes. I came a week ago."

"And you're—just walking around!"

"I don't like crowds." Her eyes moved to the house. "What a heavenly place this is!"

"Yes, Mr. Wantage is one of the lucky ones. In that respect, anyway. Here he comes. Three glasses—very thoughtful of him."

"Ice," Doyle said, "Lot's of ice." It clinked in the glass as she took it from the tray. "You were right— better than gin on a day like this."

She caught her breath. "Lovely! Worth a long, long walk."

"You should have waited till evening. Very pleasant then. I *walk*. . . . Seldom use the car. But not in heat like this."

He pulled up another chair. "If you're going into Salchurch, there are buses occasionally to Penrhuan. I suppose you've come from that direction?"

"Yes. I was telling Mr.—Smith."

"The *direct* way to Salchurch is along the coast road. You needn't have come this way at all. Unless you had some specific reason?"

It would be simpler, Smith thought, to ask for her

address and telephone number. The moving shadows of the trees touched her face. He wondered if she was beautiful or merely young and appealing. Perhaps both. . . . For once, his habit of swift analysis failed to work. He couldn't have guessed which shelf she came from, what structural concept she fitted. Permissive society turned them out like this by the score, as smooth and rootless, long-haired and long-legged, carbon-copies of some carefully synthesised original. He came up against them sometimes, especially when summer crowds filled the narrow streets of Penrhuan and the white-sanded beaches, and they worried him.

She put down the glass. "There was a reason," she said. "It doesn't matter, though. It's just a laugh. But I saw your advertisement."

Doyle Wantage frowned. "You did?"

"And I thought it would be nice to stay around here. Then I saw you in the garden and realised how ridiculous it was. Somehow I thought you'd be old."

"I'm not very young."

"But you're not *old*. . . ."

"And as I'm not old, the whole thing's ridiculous! You were walking away."

He laughed, and turned to Smith. "How's that? There's no end to the human comedy!"

There was a long silence. Smith, who knew nothing of any advertisement, concentrated on his pipe.

"It cuts both ways," Doyle said. "You expected an older man and I expected an older woman. How old are you, by the way?"

"I'm twenty-two."

She said it almost mischievously, as if humouring him, and again he glanced at the Inspector. "Wouldn't you think that twenty-two is quite young—much too young, in fact?"

"Too young for what? To be an industrial tycoon or

even a police superintendent, yes, but I don't suppose Miss—Teale has anything like that in mind. I'm in the dark about the whole thing. Have you been advertising for a wife?"

"For a housekeeper," Doyle said with some warmth. "Merely a housekeeper."

"*Merely* a housekeeper!" The Inspector seemed surprised. "I think that calls for some clarification."

"Too young," Doyle said emphatically, "and too attractive. You agree with me there?"

"I wouldn't have thought it an insuperable handicap, but it does raise points," Smith admitted.

"Now if you were sixty," Doyle said to the girl, "or I were seventy . . ."

She nodded gravely. "That's what I thought when I saw you here in the garden. But the advertisement didn't mention ages. It said you wanted a capable woman to run a small country house."

Now it was her turn to glance at the Inspector, and he saw in her face a mixture of exasperation and tolerance and bubbling fun that almost spilled into laughter. There was an instant bond between them. *What can you do,* she seemed to be saying, *with such a dear, delightful man?* And even if she had spoken the words aloud, he couldn't have told her.

"I shall frame my next advertisement more precisely," Doyle said.

"I hope you will!"

"I'm sure you're most capable, I'm sure you could run this place splendidly. But as my friend points out, you're much too young and attractive. . . ."

"I pointed out nothing of the kind," Smith said.

He began to clean out his pipe, using an old knife-blade worn down to a mere sliver of steel.

"Why should convention demand that a housekeeper must be quite lacking in the attractiveness you object to in this applicant for the post?"

"I don't object to her attractiveness at all," Doyle retorted. "On the contrary. What are you driving at?"

"A middle-aged man who brings a dour, unprepossessing woman into the house to cook meals and sew on his buttons runs little risk of scandal. He can be sure that no stones will be thrown. Morality doesn't enter into it. The arrangement is sanctified by indifference or distaste. They're made into a virtue. That's always seemed odd to me."

"Very profound!"

"I'm glad you think so."

"But in this case people *would* talk."

"No doubt they would. But morally the position would be exactly the same. I'm trying to be logical."

"One can't flout public opinion."

The Inspector was inclined to let it go at that, but Doyle Wantage had uttered the words so smugly that some protest seemed necessary.

"What else are you doing in half a dozen other directions I could mention?"

The girl's voice saved Doyle. "Is this a private argument, or could I say something? I'm *not* an applicant for the post. I was going away but you asked me to come in and have a drink."

"I apologise!" Doyle said contritely. "But the Inspector gets these bees in his bonnet. . . . Let me re-fill your glass."

"I mustn't, really . . . I ought to be going."

"I can't expect you to walk back after an abortive journey that's entirely my responsibility. You must let me take you home."

"One of those bees," said Inspector Smith, "is still buzzing. How many other replies have you had to that advertisement of yours?"

"Not one. People seemed disinclined to bury themselves in an isolated place like this."

He said it like a man with a grievance, and Smith was perfectly well aware that in spite of age-barriers and public opinion, Doyle Wantage was unwilling to let her go. He also suspected that with a little encouragement the girl would stay. But in western as well as eastern markets, one bargains to the last.

"You know what my work is?" Doyle said to her.

"Yes. I've read quite a lot about you."

That seemed to please him. "You realise why I prefer isolation?"

"Of course."

"Do you know anything about music?"

"Scarcely anything."

"That could be an advantage," Smith said, thinking aloud, and she gave him a warm smile of thanks.

"I did once go to Festival Hall," she told him.

"And you liked it?"

"Loved it. It's a wonderful building. I went with a boy who was reading architecture at London University, and he was explaining why you can't hear the trains."

Doyle rubbed his chin. "I've never been quite able to understand that myself," he said. "Could you tell me something about your background, Miss Teale?"

"I haven't one in the way you mean. Or the way I think you mean. I was born in Bristol. For two years I was a doctor's receptionist, then I went to London. I worked in a Covent Garden office and did some spare-time modelling. You know, teenage things, but there was no future in it. Not for me, anyway. Is that what you want to know?"

"It helps."

He took a few steps towards the house, then came back, frowning. "I feel inclined to compromise," he said, as if making a pronouncement on international affairs.

"True to race and upbringing!" The Inspector's burr

was kindly but pointed. "Compromise usually takes one half-way to nowhere in a long time, but it can be useful."

Doyle ignored this. His eyes were on the girl.

"You're much too thin. One thing, you'd be sure of good food and fresh air. Stay and have a meal with us. I'll think things over and give you my decision in a day or two. Will that be all right?"

"I'll have to think things over, too. And give you my decision."

"Naturally."

He shrugged into a linen jacket that had been lying on the grass. "Would you care to look over the house? I'm afraid we're lacking in modern amenities, but I'm quite willing to install anything necessary for—ha, the *dolce vita* or whatever it is. Gracious living. . . . Do you find that amusing, Mister Smith?"

"Not at all. I'm neither amused nor sceptical."

The girl, he thought, had turned a little pale, as if the heat had drained away her vitality. "There's one thing I ought to tell you—" she began, and Doyle turned attentively.

"Yes, of course. I'm afraid I've monopolised the conversation, but there's your point of view to consider. What is it?"

"It isn't a point of view," she said. "It's a fact of life. You see, I have a child."

The Inspector gently rubbed the bowl of his pipe. Though he had known Doyle Wantage since his salmon-poaching days, it was difficult to predict his reaction to this.

When it came, it was surprising. Doyle was painfully hearty.

"No need to be too sensitive about these things," he said. "I was one of a large family. Sisters galore. Smith will remember—one of them married his sergeant. I was familiar with the facts of conception and birth before I knew my alphabet. . . . Though all my sisters were on the bucolic side. Quite different from you."

Abruptly, the heartiness evaporated. "Your private life doesn't concern me. Not at all. No doubt you could arrange for the child to be taken care of?"

She shook her head. "I wouldn't want that."

"No? No, on second thoughts I'm quite sure of it. One of the reasons I would have liked to come here is that the sea is so near, and the fields all around. I'm sorry it—it all seems so impossible."

"Impossible?"

He repeated the word, apparently considering it from various angles. "I wouldn't say *impossible,* though it makes things more difficult. On the other hand, a *widow* as a housekeeper would be much nearer the norm. Oh yes, much nearer!"

"I adopted Nina soon after she was born. She's my sister's child."

"You adopted—"

"It wasn't a legal adoption. You could say that I made myself responsible for her. There was no one else to do that. I don't think the authorities could take her from me now."

A cloud-shadow had moved across the flat countryside. Its ragged edge touched the garden, momentarily dulling the brightness of lawns and flower-beds.

"You said Nina. . . . An attractive name."

"She's an attractive child."

The Inspector plucked a blade of grass and pushed it through the stem of his pipe. The cloud-shadow passed. Doyle loosened his shirt-buttons.

"Hotter than ever—don't you think so?"

No one spoke.

"Well! Well, shall we take a look at the house?"

Left alone, Inspector Smith leaned back in his chair, thinking as coherently as the weather allowed. Curious how a passing stranger can be transformed by a few random exchanges of words and ideas into a factor. Or perhaps a catalyst?

Though he wasn't sure that Doyle Wantage needed one. He could transform his own substance well enough into the stuff of art without outside help.

The thing that puzzled and sometimes dismayed Smith was the man's simplicity. For years, according to the critics, he had been moving towards some kind of maturity but had never achieved it. *This work, his most profound as yet . . . This lyrical, contemplative statement. . .*

All very well to say the hell with the critics. Surrounded by comforts of mind and body, Doyle Wantage might become still more contemplative, and Smith wasn't sure whether that would be a good thing. Like Martinu before Lidice, he probably needed the shock of emotional stimulus.

Inspector Smith, whose knowledge of such things was slight, felt mildly pleased that he could pursue the equation even that far. He settled back in the chair and closed his eyes again. Whatever else, he was far removed from criminal records. There was nothing here to remind him of envy, hatred, and malice.

Though he was reasonably certain that the mother of Nina, that attractive child, was yonder in the house with his old friend.

Doyle Wantage, since the collapse of his marriage, had been looked after by a daily woman from Salchurch village, whose progressive senility had led him to draft the advertisement. That morning she had left a salad and its accessories in the fridge. They had their meal in the garden, Doyle carrying out a table and the girl bringing the food. She was quiet and attentive, showing due respect for him, but no more.

The Inspector was not sure about her age. He would

have thought she was even younger than she claimed. What he liked about her most was her responsiveness, her warmth. He noticed it best when she laughed at one of Doyle's sallies—a joyous, unselfconscious laugh, a swift turn of her head, a tantalising fullness of her throat.

He was thinking of that when Doyle returned after taking her back to Penrhuan. Doyle was on the defensive—that was obvious as soon as he came through the gate, leaving the car on the grass verge so that he could take Smith home later. He peered down at Smith.

"Well?" he said.

"It's much cooler. I was thinking of going indoors."

"What do you think?"

"Of her, or the situation?"

"They seem to be inseparable. You like her?"

"She's presentable."

Smith got up stiffly from the chair. With the sun only just below the horizon, a light mist was already filming the fields.

Doyle took the chair from him and folded it. "In my place, what would you do?"

"I can't put myself in your place. The fires burn lower at my age, and I've fewer illusions than you have."

"About her, you mean, or are you speaking generally?"

"I was speaking generally, but if I were you I'd certainly make enquiries. You mentioned her background and she lightly sketched her history, which isn't quite the same thing. Did you see the child?"

"Yes. They're staying with Mrs. Drummond in Dale Street."

"I suppose it's occurred to you that the girl may be lying from the most understandable motives? The child may be hers."

"I've thought of that."

"The possibility doesn't worry you?"

"I don't think so. No. Why should it?"

Smith lifted his shoulders. "Why indeed? It might even simplify matters."

"What do you mean by that?"

"If this—adoption story is true, problems might crop up as time goes by. A man in your position is usually allowed a few eccentricities, but a legal battle on the eve of the Festival wouldn't do you any good."

"I've thought of that too." He folded the two remaining chairs. "Queer thing—I don't remember mentioning it before, but I always wanted a daughter."

"I don't see anything queer about it. I have one and she's a great joy to me in spite of her capers. Are you thinking of the child in that capacity, by the way, or your prospective housekeeper?"

"That's a low blow!"

"I didn't mean it to be. The point is that you didn't advertise for a daughter. You advertised for a domestic servant."

"You're striking a warning note. . . . Yes, I detect a warning note there."

They walked towards the house. It held the day's heat like an oven, in spite of wide-open windows and doors. Doyle Wantage brought beer from the kitchen and for a while they sat in silence, looking across the marsh. The big room had been made from two on the west side. It was sparsely furnished—a piano, a record-player, a few low chairs. The only picture was a Rouault, a man's head, the planes of vivid colour conventionally disposed as if the master's early work in painted glass and leaden casings had dictated its composition.

"You'll be here for the Festival?" Doyle asked.

"Not every day, I'm afraid, but as often as possible."

"I mean what I said about a hornet's nest. Cross-sections of hate and flattery, the wrangling of committees, petty jealousies and ambitions. The parson and his re-

pulsive little curate. My dear one-time wife and her
Byronic husband. Turvey for make-weight—God, it's
only by a miracle that music occasionally comes into
its own."

"You have your stalwarts," the Inspector reminded
him. "Maxton for one. I've heard you say he plays Bach
as well as anyone in the country. Will the organ be
finished in time?"

"It's finished now. One of the best things Noel Mander's ever done. Beautifully voiced, and considering
the acoustics of Luke and James that's something. Magnificent pedal—the Open is an absolute joy. The old
Snetzler ranks are housed away from the rest—gives
you the *feel* of a chamber-organ, and that's what you
need for eighteenth-century stuff."

He was in full flight. All the Inspector had to do was
listen and occasionally nod. It was quite dark by the
time Doyle finished and Smith got up to go. And inevitably, they returned to the pattern of that afternoon's
events.

"You think I'll be making a fool of myself?" Doyle
asked.

"I don't think that."

"She'll be all right here."

"I'm sure of that. But you've been alone. That makes
a difference. After so long. . . ."

"Damn it, even after so long, you don't see me creep-
ing into the girl's bed?"

"That wouldn't worry me so much. Unless I'm mistaken, you'll do something less natural."

"How do I take that?"

Smith looked across the deep-piled rug that lay between them.

"I can see you, Doyle, in that old, leather-smelling
workroom of yours on a winter night, talking to her
about your household gods. Vivaldi, Couperin, others

I wouldn't know, then putting out the light and saying goodnight to her at the door of her room and going to your own."

"Are you laughing at my stupidity or my chivalry?"

"Neither. I'm wondering how much it would cost you, that's all. It's comparatively simple to renounce earthly delights when they're not available. It can be exhausting to deny yourself when they are."

Doyle's out-thrust head moved slowly up and down. "I appreciate your point. Yes, I see what you mean. I believe you've said something quite profound."

"It seems ordinary common-sense to me."

2
Eaten Alive

Fame is an awkward wench to catch by the skirts. She twists this way and that like a frightened virgin. But when pursued more decorously she can become generous and bestowing, and sometimes comes unasked to sit by the fireside.

After the R.C.M., Doyle Wantage studied for two years in Paris, playing the piano in a left-bank café to pay his bills. During the last few months of that period he wrote the score for a documentary film, and then for Créon's *Trios Magots*. On the strength of that he went south to a village at the edge of the Camargue. Commissions were supplemented by concerts in Marseilles and Arles, and a modest tour followed. A more ambitious tour in Australia and South Africa had been arranged by his Paris agent when his father broke his back in a car-smash on the Penrhuan road. Doyle cancelled the tour, went home, and stayed with the old man till he died a month later.

Faced with actions for breach of contract, he put off his return to France so long that the spell of the far west beguiled him again. Bargehouse Mill was up for sale. He bought the place, got down to serious work, and was reaping the rewards within a year. Concert work had never greatly appealed to him, and from the day that his String Quartet was played for the first time at the Bath Festival he turned his back on it for good.

Salchurch was a modest Rural District, almost unknown except for its vast Church of St. Luke and St. James. The Festival started modestly. In those days it was Doyle Wantage's protégé, not his mistress.

Before Twelvetrees' time, the Salchurch rector was an ascetic eighty-year-old. The church was in bad repair even then. There was a Fabric Fund, fed by trickles from jumble sales, the odd bequest, an alms box placed beside the visitors' book. But when Twelvetrees took over, ominous cracks called for major repairs. And the Fabric Fund stood at twenty-four shillings.

That was when Twelvetrees approached Doyle Wantage and asked if he would arrange a fund-raising concert. Doyle was delighted. He had already gathered around him a nucleus of local talent. Rehearsals were put in hand.

The programme of that first concert is still preserved in Salchurch Festival archives. It began in the best Grand Hotel manner with *On Wings of Song* and ended, tongue in cheek, with the *Archduke.*

Funds still being low, and local talent still thirsting for recognition, other concerts followed, each slightly more austere than the last. The following year, two performances in the village hall and a recital in Luke and James were given in one week, and it could be said that the Festival had arrived.

In 1962, Bernard Sholto had completed his First Symphony and lacked an orchestra to perform it. It also happened that the New Western Orchestra, deep in the red and unable to afford accommodation in Plymouth, was looking for a hall and a conductor.

Salchurch could provide the latter. But the village hall held one hundred and eighty sitting and forty standing. And Doyle Wantage thought of the Hangar.

During the war, the Fleet Air Arm had occupied a wide tract of land north of the village. Eventually the buildings were demolished, except for one hangar that was leased to a flying club. The club had now packed up. The hangar remained, in bad repair like the church, but a possibility.

There was money to raise and official pig-headed stupidity to fight. A mountain of organisation had to be tackled almost single-handed, regulations had to be discovered and complied with. Such luxuries as heating and decor had to be forgotten till better times, but enthusiasm carried the day. On the first Saturday afternoon of September, a short Service of Dedication was held in Luke and James, and at seven-thirty that evening Doyle Wantage conducted *Cockaigne*. It was followed by the Dvorak cello concerto and the Sholto symphony.

Salchurch was a little unsure that night of the bird it had hatched, but the London critics told the simple villagers all about it next morning.

The Festival changed Salchurch. Next season, the villagers were rather less simple. They realised that the sun was shining and it was up to them to make hay. It changed the shops and the church. It brought in a trickle and then a flood of astute characters whose favourite instrument was the cash-register. Tea-shops changed into licensed restaurants with sophisticated menus. Hedges and gardens were bulldozed to provide spacious carparks behind ancient pubs.

Almost everything changed but Doyle Wantage himself. He remained aloof and unconcerned, wondering mildly what all the fuss was about.

One day shortly before the 1966 Festival was due to open, he spent ten hectic hours in the Hangar and came home as dusk was falling. There had been a heated argument with Norris Turvey, and now Doyle was thinking of all the things he should have said. Retorts that would have brought the unspeakable Turvey to his knees, casual allusions to matters beyond the Turvey ken which would have left him cowed and speechless.

The mile-long walk from Salchurch never failed to restore the balance of his sanity even when it had toppled furthest. With Turvey out of his hair, he was thinking less of the coming Festival than of the weather. For eleven months of the year he thought of September as golden, warm, misty, with cobwebs trailing from the hedges and tickling his nose as he tramped the narrow lanes. Often enough the days were anything but golden, but it was a pleasant illusion. The sky might be a dirty grey, the lanes pocked with deep puddles . . . But next year would be different. He felt grateful that accident had placed his Festival within this little span of the season he loved.

The familiar and cheerless ritual of coming home had been broken since June. No more shivering in the cold, fumbling for keys, turning on lights in an empty house. There was a welcoming glow in the stone-flagged hall. He threw his raincoat over a chest and went into the room where he worked and read and sometimes slept, that shabby, leather-smelling room Smith had mentioned. The lamp above his table was turned on. She had not heard him come in. She was kneeling in front of his books, running her finger along the shelves.

He closed the door and she turned quickly.

"Did I startle you?" he asked.

"I didn't expect you yet. You said it might be midnight." Her smile had a frank, unaffected warmth. He thought she was glad he was early.

"Most of that's technical stuff. You'll get lost." He knelt beside her and took a grey-backed book from another shelf. "Have a go at this. A friend of mine wrote it."

He found a pipe among the litter of papers on the table. "It's been a hell of a day," he said. "Trying company. My ex-wife, who's pure vixen. Her present husband, who has a rabbit's timidity without its charm.

And a wolfish character called Turvey. You haven't met them yet. You will, given time."

She was turning the leaves of the book he had given her. "It's about *why* people like me make music," he said. "Not how."

"May I take it and read it?"

"You can read it without taking it anywhere. Don't you think it's cold in here?" Logs were laid in the open fireplace. He struck matches and reached for the brass-bound bellows in the corner. "I've work to do tonight."

"You're sure I won't disturb you?"

He got up from his knees. "Some people would, but not you. Nina's in bed, I suppose?"

"Long ago."

"Did you ring Brodericks about that roof?"

"They're sending a man next week."

"So we live in the pious hope that it doesn't rain till then! If it does, bring her down and we'll put her in another room. You too. You can't be up there under a leaking roof."

He sat down at the table and worked steadily till nearly midnight. Long hours of work had weakened his eyes. When he hooked off his heavy spectacles, his head was aching violently. She was watching him, her eyes steady and concerned above the book.

"Would you like some coffee, Mr. Wantage?"

"Please."

When she had gone, he stared down at the rampantly annotated pages. In the course of time he would enjoy the fruits, but there was ploughing and harrowing to be done in this job as in any other. He was all but asleep when she came back. She had her own way, a good way, of making coffee. He watched her pouring it—thick strong stuff.

"Where's your cup?" he asked.

"In the kitchen."

"Do you prefer drinking your coffee there?"

She looked up at him. "No."

"Then why do you? I don't ask you to stay with me all evening and then dismiss you like a paid servant."

"I am a paid servant."

"Oh Christ," he burst out, "do you have to be so damned sorry for yourself?"

"That, from *you!*" she said.

"A paid servant is only part of what you are. Bring that cup."

With a shrug of her shoulders, she went to the kitchen and brought it. He pulled a low chair towards the fire for her.

"So you think I'm the self-pitying one?"

"I don't really. But you made me furious when you said that. Can't you understand how conscious I am of the way we're here together?"

"You must be," he said. "I know you are, and I fall over backwards trying to make it up to you. Sorry I slipped up tonight. I'm damn tired, Jan."

"Don't do any more tonight. Go to bed."

He shook his head. "I'm damn tired because of all the stuff churning around in my head. Mostly rubbish. I wouldn't sleep. Talking rests me more than sleeping does. Let's make a wake of it for another hour and I'll sleep like an old dog."

He lay back in the chair. "On the last night of the Festival," he told her, "I shall give a small supper-party here. There'll be distinguished men accompanied by their undistinguished wives, plus a few of our native oafs and termagants. I've done it before with the help of Shilstone caterers. This time I'd like you to take care of it. Are you willing to try?"

"I'm willing to try."

"You can have whatever help you need. If we're short of household fal-de-lals, get them. And when the time comes, you won't stay in the kitchen. You'll sit beside me. Is that clear?"

"I'll think it over."

There were various things he could have said, or done, in those moments of warmth. She had a score of vulnerable points, and by now he knew them all. But he played safe, aware of his own weaknesses.

Already, he'd committed himself a good deal further than he should. He knew quite well that the row he'd had with Turvey had been over the girl. Grace too was sharpening her claws. Grace had been a bitch when he was married to her and she was still. She too had known his weaknesses, and played upon them unmercifully. He only had to think of that grey-backed book he had given Janice to read. Young Carlin had written it—beautiful, sensitive stuff. He had been very close to Carlin. Not his cleverest student, but certainly his most discriminating one. Grace had interpreted their closeness in her own way, her bent way. Janice Teale would come out of it even worse. Grace—with Turvey at her elbow as usual—had hinted only that evening that Doyle's morals, of course, were his own affair, and anyway who cared nowadays, but wasn't he rather down-grading himself? Turvey had appreciated that.

Doyle flexed his fingers. Like many gentlemen, he sometimes dreamed of violence. . . . And the seeds of violence were thick in Salchurch. Without Grace and the execrable Turvey, how pleasant the Festival would be! But that was a thought one pushed back into the libido or wherever it came from.

She brought him back from the shadows by asking what he was working on now.

"Something that may see daylight at next year's Festival. Partly choral—unusual for me."

"I'm learning. Slowly, very slowly. . . . Until I came here, I'd always thought of a composer working at a piano."

"Picking out bits and pieces, yes. It must be a great

help if one can, but it's a trick I never picked up."

He was gently mocking, but it went over her head. "Those films—"

"I know. I usually come out. Or turn it off if it's a television one. I believe doctors do when a Hollywood surgeon starts delving around in someone's viscera."

He laughed derisively. "The girl with her elbow on the piano, and the composer who gazes up at her instead of keeping his eyes on the job. Inevitably he's like poor doomed Schubert or the young Liszt. Curious, that. . . . Some of the beefiest men I know are composers. Is it two bars or three before she breaks in to tell him it's wonderful?"

"Two," she said. "At the third she starts to sing words by Al Guzzelberger and Chuck Sauerkraut."

"And at the sixth they're joined by the Hollywood Basin Orchestra, all one hundred and twenty pieces of it. What are pieces—d'you know?"

Smiling, she moved the brown coffee-pot nearer the fire.

"Now you know the truth," he said. "Your composer is a dour, unromantic craftsman who writes his music at an old table in a shabby room, as prosaically as if he were filling in his tax-returns."

"Are we off the lunatic fringe now? Can I ask a reasonable question?"

"You can."

"Do you *hear* it as you write it down?"

He gave her a long, quizzical look.

"You feel a thing, experience it, you can be permeated by it. You understand? Hearing—that's different. When we say we see a thing in our mind's eye, what do we mean? I don't know of any screen at the back of my skull. When we hear a thing that doesn't make sound—I don't know."

He picked up a worn tobacco-pouch. "What's the difference between brain and mind? I don't know. You'd better go to bed before we get too involved."

She thoughtfully drew a long strand of hair through her fingers, then tossed it back over her shoulder. "Ebor Maxton talks about *seeing.*"

"Like a terrier with a bone, aren't you? Never give up! One can never be quite sure with Maxton."

"Is he really, totally blind?"

"He has plastic eyeballs. You can't be blinder than that."

"He came this afternoon—I almost forgot to tell you. How does he find his way around with so little trouble?"

"Partly because of the mysteries we've just been discussing, partly because his remaining senses are abnormally acute. He always cuts along Willow Walk when he goes home from this end of the village. I wouldn't go that way in the dark if it saved twice the distance. Six feet of water in the creek and a footpath less than a yard wide. But he thinks nothing of it. Did he leave any message?"

"He would like you to ring him before nine in the morning."

"I wonder why he came?" Doyle frowned. "I know he had an argument with Turvey—"

"He didn't mention that."

"He wouldn't, to you. You like Ebor Maxton, don't you?"

"I—yes, I think I do. Though I'm not sure I would if I knew him better. He likes to impress upon you that no one's necessary to him and he wouldn't much care if the human race was blotted out."

"That's his defence mechanism in operation. There are times when he carries it too far and makes himself ridiculous."

"He did today," she said, and Doyle waited with interest. "He'd bought a record—a clarinet quintet by Brahms."

"You're making giant strides. One day I may make you my secretary."

"I *won't* be drawn, Mr. Wantage. . . . It had a beautiful sleeve. A garden scene—a girl leaning against a wall, with rose-beds all around and a sloping lawn like ours."

"Ours, yes!"

"I *won't* rise to the bait, Mr. Wantage—I WON'T, not even if you dangle the juiciest fly! I made some remark about the sleeve and he said he really hadn't taken a good look at it. I felt a complete fool."

"No doubt he intended that you should."

"Then I mentioned the roses, and he asked about the girl's dress—what colour was it? I said yellow, and he nodded and said that would look nice against the green lawn. It's rather frightening, I think."

"He probably transposes colour into some other sensual idiom. You're meeting some queer fish, aren't you? And there are plenty more in the tank. Grace for one— I shall enjoy hearing your opinion of her when you meet."

"She was your wife."

"That doesn't make her a sacred cow. Have you never wondered why she still has so much to do with the way the Festival's run?"

"Has that anything to do with me?"

He knew quite well that it hadn't. She had told him little enough about her own affairs, and probably his were of small interest to her. But he felt in some odd way that he had to justify himself. Ebor Maxton was not the only one with a well-developed defence mechanism.

"As my wife," he said, "she was secretary of the Festival Association. She still is. I couldn't very well ask her to resign when she married Heneage Iles."

He reached for her cup, but she shook her head. "No more tonight—it would keep me awake. . . . You're not a very assertive man, Mr. Wantage."

"I've always disliked the idea of being. I've known so many assertive men and detested them all. Fortunately the balance will come down on my side this weekend. You remember Smith? We shall be seeing him on Saturday."

He gathered the papers together and stuffed them into a briefcase. "And now I'm going to bed. Tomorrow's another day. General committee meeting at ten-thirty. And old Twelvetrees wants some assurances about our use of Luke and James. Apparently Norris Turvey's got on the wrong side of him and I'll have to restore order. If I have to take sides with Turvey it will be most reluctantly. He's one of the assertive characters I dislike."

He listened, head on one side. "Rain?"

Janice went to the window. "It is. Quite heavy, too."

"What did I say? Those blasted tiles! What's Broderick's number?"

"You can't ring him at midnight! He'll be in bed."

"And I hope it's raining in on him. Anyway, I'd better take a look at that ceiling. Leave all these things till morning."

"No, I'll clear away later. I hate to see last night's dirty dishes when the milk comes."

They went upstairs.

The steps were wide and shallow, leading to a half-landing with a tall window, now splashed with rain and rattling in the sudden wind. From the upper landing, a narrower staircase led to the top floor.

"With four spare rooms on the floor below," Doyle Wantage said, leading the way, "there was no need to banish yourself up here at all."

"But I like it. There's a heavenly view over the marsh."

The wooden-floored corridor in that top range creaked under their feet. She opened the door quietly, and he saw the gleam of new paintwork. The child lay on a single bed in the corner, her face grave and still under the shaded light.

Doyle pushed his hands deep into his pockets. A lot had happened during these past three months. At first, they had been as formal with each other as if indeed he was the septuagenarian she had expected to see, and she the most respectable widow. Things were different now. No longer did she automatically agree with all he said; they argued fiercely about a dozen subjects. She never troubled now to hide her moods. Neither did he. She was friend and disciple and critic of his disorganised existence, she ran the house like a machine and was devoted to his comforts.

But he had never asked her, never thought of asking her, if the child was hers. It was something he didn't understand, a wary suspicion that the fruit of the tree of knowledge often has a bitter kernel.

"It isn't exactly dripping yet." She pointed to the ceiling. "But you can see the patch."

"I'll have it done tomorrow. If Broderick can't come we'll find someone else. . . . You've made this old place cosy! How on earth have you managed to do it?"

"You said I could use anything I could find on the top floor. So I rummaged. There are some lovely bits and pieces."

He bent over the bed. "Like you, she shows a marked preference for my room. If you miss any of her things, you'll probably find them in the cupboard where I keep my manuscript paper."

"But I'd no idea! She plays around the house and in the garden, of course—it's quite safe when the gate's closed. I won't let her disturb you any more."

"She doesn't, any more than you do. She comes in through the window, by the way. It's rather funny to see her squirming through. Insinuating herself, her eyes on me, wondering if it's all right."

He glanced back from the door. "I always wanted a daughter. I remember saying that to Smith when he was here."

She followed him out of the room. "Didn't Grace want children?" she asked abruptly.

"I don't know." He leaned against the stair-rail. "May seem a damn stupid thing to say, but there it is. To Grace, sex was indispensable but reproduction indelicate. I don't think she ever equated the two. I doubt if she even associated them. I believe there are women of certain primitive tribes even now who don't relate their expanding proportions with what happened at the Feast of the Young Men."

"Do you have to be so cynical about it? Anyway, you can't tell me that Grace—"

"Oh God, I'm merely speaking in parables! I'm trying to say that she kept cause and effect in strictly separate compartments. I don't think much about it now. It seems a long time ago."

Her fingers were still on the door-handle. He slowly turned his head. "Why should I talk to you like this?"

"I suppose there must be some reason."

"Do you mind?"

"No."

"I met her in London. An orchestra that folded long ago. She was its librarian. Academic, methodical. . . . In those days I had a healthy respect for the *intelligentsia*. That's a label for those people who know all the notes. Nothing else—the notes. I slept with her that night. I remember thinking that it was bloody good— that a few years of it would be bloody good. You see?"

"But it didn't last as long as that?"

"Three months!" He listened to the rain, to the uneasy sound of the wind. "They taught me a lot. I found out what it meant to be *used*. Often enough it's the other way round. Plenty of women are used. But for a man, I think, it's worse. *Used,* like a spider. God Almighty, it's like being eaten alive."

He straightened his back and went carefully down the stairs. "Ah well, Heneage Iles is the spider now, poor devil! *He's* being eaten alive. Gobbled, digested—eaten alive."

She followed him down. "I'll clear away now, Mr. Wantage."

"I shouldn't have said all this."

"Why not?"

"You never talk about your experiences. Or your problems, if you have any."

"I have them. Some day—yes, some day I'll tell you about them."

He stood aside to let her pass. "When is it your birthday, Jan?"

"In November. The seventh."

"You shall have a cake with twenty-three candles, and I'll give you twenty-three pounds to buy something. You could go to Plymouth. Or even to London."

"I wouldn't want to do that. I'll spend it in Shilstone."

"Perhaps we could go together. A meal, a drink. . . ."

"Yes, I'd like that."

He listened again. "That roof worries me. . . . Don't stay up too long."

"I won't."

"By the way, I didn't lock the front door."

"You never do." She gave him a quick smile. "I'll see to it. Goodnight."

He stood just inside his bedroom door. He heard the click of the front latch, then the sound of water running in the kitchen. He looked up at the ceiling. Then, very slowly and thoughtfully, he began to wind his watch.

3

Lieblich Piccolo

At one o'clock, Inspector Smith left Sergeant Strake in charge of the Shilstone police station and walked across the Square to the Poltimore Arms, where they put on a cheese-and-beer ploughman's lunch that usually fortified him until his evening meal. As he grew older, high summer was the season he liked least in the Penrhuan district. Every year, more and more people came. Driving offences, petty crime, a suicide that had worried him more than he cared to admit—it would be pleasant when the last visitor had gone, when the gulls were once again in undisputed possession of the rock-strewn coves.

From the back bar he could see into the lounge, got up in chrome and plastic to make the tourists feel at home. And who should be there but young Aumbrey, dog-collar and all, Twelvetrees's curate from Salchurch.

It gave the last of Smith's cheese an unpleasant flavour. Worse, Aumbrey had seen him, and was edging towards the communicating door with smooth, plump hand raised in greeting.

It was too late to escape. "You do remember me?" Aumbrey asked. "Wantage brought you down to see Luke and James. Or am I mistaken? No, not possibly!"

The Inspector unwillingly returned the greeting, and Aumbrey, a glass of light ale in his free hand, called the barmaid to fill up Smith's tankard. He believed in being all things to all men, even infidels; his habit of calling in this pub and that was part of a carefully-developed back-slapping technique.

Wantage had been caustic about him. Aumbrey was neither simpering nor sanctimonious. There was something about him more deadly than that, a professionalism that would make him a bishop in time. He was slightly below average height, and with his beautiful teeth and eyes had the look of an overgrown choirboy. *Don't be deceived,* Doyle had said, *he's the most dangerous repository for gossip and scandal for twenty miles around.*

"You're coming over for the Festival?" he asked.

"I'm hoping to see—or hear—something of it," Smith said guardedly.

"The district owes a great deal to Wantage."

"I agree with you."

His eyes moved critically over Smith. An inspector of police should surely cut a more impressive figure. Aumbrey doubted whether his faded uniform was less than ten years old.

"How coincidental that we should find ourselves in the same pub!" he said. "Though as a policeman, you probably don't believe in coincidence?"

Smith snapped open his thin-bladed knife. "It comes to my rescue occasionally."

"I often think that Wantage is a victim of his own genius." Aumbrey drank delicately. "You know what I mean?"

"I'm not sure that I do."

"I was referring to his intellectual integrity. Unfortunately it doesn't preserve him from the devious machinations of such people as Maxton and Turvey. Not to mention his ex-wife and her present husband."

Smith stirred uncomfortably. "Wantage is an old friend of mine," he said. "But he doesn't discuss his personal problems with me."

"Personally, I *revere* him as an artist and as a man. But one can't shut one's eyes to the loves and hates, the ambitions, the greed and lust and power-complexes inseparable from any group of people who concern themselves with anything as complex and controversial as the Festival."

He took a deep breath, as though the involved statement had almost exhausted his powers. While Smith nodded as if he understood perfectly.

"The point I'm trying to make, Inspector, is that Salchurch is not only the home of an elect and exclusive circle, but the pest-house of their lackeys and hangers-on."

"Like the poor," ventured Smith in his soft burr, "they're always with us. I've met Maxton, of course. I wouldn't have thought he was involved in any—machinations against Wantage."

"Outwardly, no! But I mistrust him. Brilliant fellow, but still . . . He's overcome his handicap so magnificently that one is scarcely aware of it. One sometimes thinks that sight would be superfluous to him."

"A curious name!" the Inspector said. "I don't remember coming across it before. Ebor Maxton—very odd!"

"I've heard him claim that he was conceived in a third-class railway-carriage *en route* to Halifax after a race-meeting in York," Aumbrey said blandly, with his choirboy smile.

"That should have given him a useful start," Smith said, equally bland.

The curate dismissed Ebor. "Then, of course, we have Turvey . . . Who was quite recently involved in a most amusing incident at Luke and James. Amusing or bizarre, as one sees it."

Inspector Smith felt that he was in an embarrassing position. All his instincts urged him to snub Aumbrey and walk out. . . . But he had a professional interest in odd people and their odd ways. Doyle Wantage had hinted, in June, that there were disturbing undercurrents in Salchurch. There seemed no point in closing his ears to information which might just possibly be useful.

"Norris Turvey," pursued Aumbrey, "is director and general manager of an electrical utilities factory. One who can be relied upon for a thousand-pound bond, and therefore chairman of the Festival Finance Committee. Completely under the influence of Wantage's ex-wife, and probably providing her with the sexual stimulus her present husband fails to supply."

"Her present husband being Heneage Iles, I believe?"

"Words fail me, Inspector! Handsome as Lucifer, crafty as a rat! A would-be patron of the arts, one of the few men in Salchurch who neither toil nor spin."

"She seems to be in an enviable position. A present husband of wealth, a discarded one of fame, with an alternative to both if she chooses. I never met her when she was Wantage's wife, but if your estimate isn't too biased I should image him well rid of her."

"But he isn't rid of her."

Aumbrey was very emphatic. "Not by any means! Grace Iles still manages her ex-husband's life to a very considerable extent. Secretary to the Festival Association and a member of the Advisory Board—oh yes, she's quite a power behind the throne. Naturally the arrangement leads to constant friction. . . . And between ourselves, Inspector, this unfortunate housekeeper business doesn't help."

It was thrown out just a trifle too casually. Aumbrey probably hoped that it would be taken up. But Inspector Smith chose to ignore it.

"These things usually find their own level," he said. "I imagine that most people will be too busy with the Festival to air their personal grievances."

"One hopes so. Certainly Wantage will. I wish him

every success. Especially with his own work, his *magnum opus*. It will be a moving occasion for him, even if incomprehensible to the rest of us. *Tantae molis erat!* A fitting title for a work which has occupied him for so long."

Inspector Smith made a mental note to look up his daughter's *Foreign Phrases and Classical Quotations* when he got home, and took another long pull at his beer.

The nearby church bells chimed the half-hour. Smith checked his watch, aware that Aumbrey was watching him, so closely that he wondered for a moment if there was some hidden purpose behind his meanderings.

"You mentioned an amusing incident in connection with Turvey."

"Amusing or bizarre—I think those were my words." The watchful expression had left Aumbrey's face; it was blandly ingenuous again. "It must have been extremely unpleasant. If Warbleton had not providentially arrived when he did, it could have been worse."

He peered into Smith's tankard, but it was still half-full. The Inspector was an abstemious man.

"Warbleton is verger of Luke and James. He told reporters that on the morning in question he came to the church early and began to dust and polish in preparation for the Holier than Thous."

"I beg your pardon?"

"The Mothers' Union. We lesser clergy grovel lower in mortal terror before that hatchet-faced brigade than we do before our bishops. Warbleton had heard strange sounds on entering, but put them down to bats and birds and the contractions of this and the expansion of that which hot weather induces in old buildings. However, the noise started up again. He described it as a yammering, accompanied by a high-pitched whistle."

Aumbrey paused for effect. The Inspector was hanging upon his words in a most flattering manner.

"He eventually traced this medley of sounds to the organ, Ebor Maxton's pride and joy and Mr. Noel Mander's most recent triumph. It is housed in a chamber above the chancel and played from a console in the choir-stalls some sixty feet away. It is approached by a winding stone staircase which formerly gave access to the rood-screen, and at the foot of this staircase a very solid door has been fitted. Do I make myself clear?"

"As a witness," the Inspector said, "you would be invaluable."

"You may never have explored the interior of a big organ? A complication of boxes, wind-chests, electro-pneumatic apparatus, staircases and ladders! Warbleton discovered first that the blower had been left on. Next, that the organ's interior lighting, controlled by a switch outside the door, had been turned off. The high-pitched whistle beat him, but it was later shown that it was a cipher . . . a note that has gone down, so to speak, but hasn't come up again. Most important of all, some luckless human was inside the organ and had apparently been there all the night."

"Norris Turvey?" suggested Smith.

"Precisely, though Warbleton was not aware of that fact till a little later. He ran to Maxton's house, where Ebor was taking his bath. They both went back to Luke and James, Maxton unlocked the organ, and a very hungry and angry Norris Turvey greeted them."

"An incredible thing!" The Inspector was frankly interested now. "What had led up to it?"

Aumbrey smirked. "Turvey's story was that he entered the church on Festival business the previous evening, when Maxton was rehearsing a forthcoming recital. Hearing the cipher and being an electrical expert as well as an amateur of music, he climbed to the organ chamber. He could have spared himself the trouble. With the organ recently completed and the

Festival coming on, the builders were expected down
to rectify just such trivial matters as that. But while
there, the lights went out and he heard the bang of
the door below. He says that he shouted, but the cipher
was squealing and the blower running, and when he
hurried towards the staircase he struck his head on a
projection and was unconscious for a minute or so."

"During which Maxton left the church?"

"He did. So when Turvey came round he was faced
with the prospect of twelve hours at least in total darkness and a piercing whistle a few feet above his head.
Warbleton says that Turvey was cut and bruised and
looked like a man who has been in the jungle for a
week. You see, he's claustrophobic, and after an hour
or so he became—restive."

He repeated the word, rolling it round his tongue
as if it gave him satisfaction. "Restive and then desper-
ate. If the Luke and James organ had been on solid
ground, he could have shifted the pipes and clambered
through to freedom. But a twenty-foot jump into the
chancel was a different matter. He told me that he
tried to locate the offending cipher. A thankless task!
It was a diminutive pipe in the *leiblich piccolo* rank,
high up in an enclosed section of the choir organ."

"What was Maxton's version of the affair?" Smith
asked.

"Ebor's? Oh, quite straightforward! He was putting
in an hour's practice in the cool of the evening. Yes,
he knew that the organ door was open. A party of
schoolchildren had come to Luke and James that afternoon, and he had taken one or two of the seniors up
the steps to show them the works. The upper limits
of his hearing stop short just below the frequency of
the cipher, and he never dreamed that Turvey was
in the organ or even in the church. So when about to
leave, he crossed the chancel and locked the door. He
also remembers turning off the light. He heard no one

call. As for the blower, he claims that he forgot to turn it off and to cancel the *lieblich piccolo* stop."

"All of which may be quite true," the Inspector said.

"Quite true. Though highly unlikely."

Inspector Smith reflected with some complacency that it was no affair of his. Unlikely things do happen. On the other hand, it was the sort of trick Ebor Maxton would delight in, especially if the victim was someone he disliked. And Smith found it hard to believe that Maxton's hearing-range was limited. Maxton had sometimes claimed that he saw with his ears.

Aumbrey caught the barmaid's eye, but Smith shook his head. "No, no—I allow myself one half-pint at lunchtime. I've already exceeded that by a hundred per cent."

Aumbrey took it gracefully. But he seemed to realise that time was almost up. He moistened his lips with a pink tongue.

"There's another matter," he said.

For the first time, he seemed to notice the Inspector's eyes. "I must say," he went on, "that I've been hoping to meet you. Do you know Wantage's housekeeper?"

"I met her once. And if you're about to ask my opinion of her age and her relationship with Wantage, I'd rather not talk about it."

"I hope I'm broad-minded, Inspector . . ."

"I hope you are. Though I thought the clergy interpreted broad-mindedness as charity. Or am I behind the times?"

Aumbrey avoided the pitfall. "I met her—once. Not at Wantage's house, but in the dead of night, half-way along Salchurch Lane. And it was probably a lucky encounter—for her."

Smith put down his tankard. "I think you'd better explain."

"I'm glad to have aroused your interest at last, Inspec-

tor. . . . Twelvetrees had a slight disagreement with
Wantage about the use of Luke and James, and I was
sent to make peace between them. It was about half-
past ten, a week ago last Tuesday night, when I drove
towards Bargehouse Mill. Wantage had indicated that
he would be working till then. My lights picked out
the figure of a woman, walking, I might almost say stum-
bling, along the strip of grass between the lane and
the creek. I stopped the car and asked if I could help."

He smiled, well satisfied with the impression he was
making. "Talking is thirsty work," he said. "Sure you
won't, Inspector?"

"All right—this once. But I haven't much time to
spare."

With glass and tankard refilled, Aumbrey leaned back
expansively against the counter.

"I asked if she'd lost her way, if she'd been attacked,
perhaps. She said no, she wasn't feeling well, she had
stumbled and fallen. I thought that was untrue. It might
have accounted for her torn dress and the bruise on
her face, but she was literally shaking with fear, and
I couldn't imagine a mere fall accounting for that. I
asked if I might take her home, wherever she lived,
and mentioned that I was on my way to Bargehouse
Mill. She astounded me by saying that she was Doyle
Wantage's housekeeper, and asked me to say nothing
to him about the incident."

The choirboy smile lit his face again. "What do you
make of that, Inspector?"

"It seems puzzling."

"I thought so. I asked if she had left the house without
her employer's knowledge, but she replied that he
never interfered with her movements and she was always free to come and go as she chose. But with the
Festival approaching, Mr. Wantage already had more
than enough to worry him, and she had no wish to
increase his anxieties."

."That seems reasonable enough."

"So far as it goes, yes. But it didn't end there. What happened was even more disturbing than Turvey's experience in Luke and James. Let me explain! The lane is very narrow and badly surfaced. When first I saw the girl, she was walking along the right-hand verge. I stopped my car on the left side, naturally, and crossed the lane to her. The conversation I have just recounted took place there. I was wondering what to say next when another car came towards us from the direction of Wantage's house. It was coming along very fast, and the sight of it—or its headlights, for that was all one could see—had a quite alarming effect upon the girl."

Smith waited. Aumbrey, he thought, was doing well.

"She seized the sleeve of my coat and literally dragged me towards the ditch. That probably saved my life—and I assure you, Inspector, that I am not exaggerating. There was scarcely room for him to pass, with my own car parked across the lane. One would have thought that he would have slowed down or stopped. But he did neither. He hit the grass verge and passed within a foot of us as we crouched on the bank of the ditch."

The Inspector's habit of interrogation asserted itself.

"Did you recognise the car?"

"My dear Inspector! It was a dark night with a slight drizzle of rain. I saw nothing with any certainty but the lights. I had the impression that it was a big car, but nothing more than that."

"You must have thought a good deal about it since then, Mr. Aumbrey. Perhaps you've reached some conclusion?"

"For what it's worth, yes. For some reason she had been to the village. Someone offered her a lift to Bargehouse Mill. She accepted. Then for *some reason* she was forced to leave the car or thrown out. An alternative is that she was walking back when someone tried to run her down. Then the driver went on to the only possible turning-point near Bargehouse Mill and drove back to finish the job."

It was a possibility. Smith thought it over but kept other possibilities within sight.

"You've no proof," he said, "that the girl had been knocked down before you arrived on the scene. The car you saw may have been driven back towards Salchurch from some place beyond the turning-point at Bargehouse Mill."

"From what place, Inspector? Certainly you can get through from the Shilstone road. But beyond Wantage's house the lane deteriorates into a mere track. No one would drive that way when it's no nearer than the main road. As for your doubts about what happened before I came along, I went back next morning to investigate. There were two sets of tyre-tracks on the grass verge. I'm not accomplished in detection, but I feel certain that they were made by the same car. They were about a hundred yards apart. The first set were probably made when the driver tried to run the girl down—I'm confident that happened though I did mention alternatives. The second were made when he came so near to running us both down."

"You haven't reported this, I take it?"

"No. I mentioned it to Twelvetrees. He said that considering the girl's position and the approach of the Festival, the less said the better. . . . Though he did suggest that you should be told—off the record."

"Kind of him! I've no jurisdiction in Salchurch and he should well know that. It's Dymond's territory."

Aumbrey nodded. "And Superintendent Dymond runs it from St. Petroch. He leaves such things to Donald and Makepeace. And the three have as little imagination between them as a rabbit."

"You'd need a good deal more than imagination to pick up the scent now, Mr. Aumbrey. A week ago last

Tuesday! Did you take the girl back to Bargehouse Mill?"

"I did. She'd pulled herself together remarkably well by the time we got there. She excused herself and made for the kitchen quarters. By the time she brought in coffee half an hour later there was nothing to show for her adventure but a bruise on her face. I noticed that she was careful to conceal it from Wantage."

It was as dead as yesterday's news, of course. And in any case it was no concern of Smith's. His own boundaries were wide enough without poaching on Dymond's preserves. But it concerned Wantage; it wasn't something he could shrug off.

"You may not have been Doyle Wantage's only visitor that night," he said. "There may after all be an innocent explanation, except for the driver's criminal behaviour when he so nearly ran you down. The girl may have slipped and fallen."

Aumbrey's smile was maddeningly superior. "That did occur to me. But I diplomatically enquired about that from Wantage. I *was* his only visitor that night."

4
Out of Hand

Smith liked to keep a few days' leave in hand, so that he could get away with a clear conscience when occasions like the Salchurch Festival came round. Doyle Wantage had called twice at the cramped Shilstone police-station during August. Two of his sisters still lived nearby, and though they avoided any truck with Salchurch and his musical career he liked to keep in touch with them. He had asked Smith to come over on the Friday evening, when a few of the Festival personalities would be dropping in. The Inspector's wife would also be most welcome, he added. . . .

But Mrs. Smith was preparing for their daughter's wedding, arranged for mid-September, and he resigned himself to the prospect of going alone.

"Why not make a weekend of it," Doyle suggested," "instead of coming back the same night?"

It was an attractive idea. He thought it over for a week, satisfied himself that crime in Penrhuan was on the wane, briefed Sergeant Strake and Constable Maen, and sent his best suit to the cleaners.

The Inspector had never owned a car, though occasionally he drove the venerable police vehicle in which Strake patrolled the neighbourhood. On Friday afternoon, September the ninth, raincoat over his arm, pipe going well, carrying a weekend bag, he walked down to the Penrhuan bus station. It was very warm. Golden sunlight bathed the little town, there was a light mist over the sea. Thunder had been mentioned. He hoped it would hold off at least until the Festival had got under way.

The bus put him down in the Square at Salchurch, which was not a square at all, but a triangle with mellow Georgian houses on all of its three sides, and a central garden studded with fine trees. Doyle had driven in to meet him.

"You did say it was an informal affair tonight," Smith said to him. "I'm not one for social occasions."

"It won't be one. People just drop in. Nothing's ever arranged. Ebor Maxton will almost certainly be there."

"And Turvey?"

"Not tonight, thank God. He's in Zurich."

"For the duration of the Festival?"

"That would be too much to pray for. No, I had a letter from him this morning, apologising for non-attendance at a meeting of the Finance Committee. He mentioned that he'd be flying back early tomorrow."

There were other questions the Inspector could have asked. Doyle Wantage had never mentioned his housekeeper since that scorching June evening. *Now,* he was saying, *come and see.* It was tempting to make a casual enquiry. Doyle, in fact, might be expecting that. But Smith had a high opinion of silence in the right places.

"So you have Tennier conducting," he said.

"For the second year, yes. First-class, of course, but not the man I would have chosen."

"Then who did choose him?"

Doyle turned out of the main street into Salchurch Lane. "The Committee," he said.

Smith nodded. "That's the way it goes. These things get out of hand. Like children, they grow. And like children they sometimes renounce their parentage. How does Ebor Maxton get along with Tennier?"

"He doesn't. He says Tennier is a show-off and a self-opinionated bastard."

Smith gave a dry chuckle. "I wouldn't wonder if Tennier's opinion of Maxton is much the same. Still, I like him."

They had left the sparse scattering of houses behind and were running along the dyke road. It must have been somewhere near this spot that Aumbrey had shared his curious adventure with Janice Teale. The road was raised a foot or so above the surrounding fields. The Inspector noticed, with a small sense of loss, that the barley had been harvested. Swaying in the wind, it had seemed a part of those summer days.

It was not the only change. The creeper on the walls of Bargehouse Mill was turning gold and red. There were other differences about the place, less easy to define. It was more than new paint and curtains, less tangible than the welcome of firelight. They swung across the gravel-sweep and he got out, waiting till Doyle extricated his long legs. The door opened as they turned towards the porch-steps.

It was a moment of boyish triumph for Doyle, and Smith did nothing to spoil it. She was different too. Cooler and more self-possessed, long hair brushed smooth, sheened with strands of copper and gold. It was a difficult moment. Smith in his time had seen the harvest of many follies, and he thought that Doyle Wantage had possibly committed the most monumental folly of all. But with the girl smiling up at him, it was difficult to be cynical.

"I'm very glad to see you here," he said.

"And I'm glad to be here."

Doyle put his weekend bag at the foot of the stairs. "If you'll excuse me, I want to phone Twelvetrees. Jan will take care of you."

Smith nodded. Doyle Wantage, he thought, had carefully rehearsed that.

He picked up the bag before Janice could reach it. "By Wantage's appearance," he said, "you've been feeding him well. He's lost that haggard look."

She laughed. "I try. . . . Though sometimes it's difficult to persuade him to eat anything at all. Let me take you up to your room."

He followed her upstairs. The room smelt of fresh linen and chrysanthemums. He looked round, his eyes alight with pleasure. "Even the flowers!" he said.

The window looked across the level expanse of marsh towards the sea. He could see the coastline, rising to the Penrhuan heights. The Ness lighthouse gleamed like a yellow candle-flame through the haze.

He glanced at the bedside table. "The books, too."

"Mr. Wantage helped me there. He told me you're an unsophisticated person with very good taste."

"Charming of him! I haven't thought about it much, but he could be right. And I do appreciate that you troubled to ask him."

He was still trying to pin her down, though without much success. A little less thin. . . . Which made her even more attractive. A curious mixture of sensuousness and innocence. Happy, he thought, but in a guarded way, a watchful way. Happy, perhaps, because she was giving Doyle Wantage as much as she took from him, and that gave her the poise and assurance which she lacked that summer afternoon three months ago.

"What are you thinking?" she asked.

"That you've changed."

"I'm older. A quarter of a year older."

"Yes, and miracles can happen in less time than that. What about your little girl?"

"She's very happy."

"I'd like to see her."

"You shall. . . . We have a room just above this one. Though she never stays there. She's always in the garden, or with Mr. Wantage in his room when we're alone."

"Alone? Oh yes, I understand! You mean when you

and Mr. Wantage are not afflicted with visitors."

She closed the window. "He's very good to her."

"And to you?"

She looked at him for a moment before the smile crossed her face. "And to me."

He nodded. "I can believe that. It must give you great satisfaction."

"You mean the fact that he's good to me?"

"Not quite that. But when you remember the chaos in which he lived before you came . . ."

"There are other kinds of chaos than untidy rooms and dishes in the sink," she said evenly.

"Things you can't clear up so easily, you mean?"

She went to the door. "I'll bring up a cup of tea for you in a few minutes, Mr. Smith."

He sat down near the window, thinking of Aumbrey and his odd story. She brought up the tea but stayed only a moment to tell him that Maxton was on his way—the Rector had seen him and reported to Doyle.

"You have an efficient grape-vine," he said.

"Sometimes too efficient . . . Will you be hungry before they've all gone home? If you are, slip into the kitchen and I'll make something for you. Nobody will notice—Ebor Maxton talks and *talks*. . . ."

He sat there till it was quite dark. Turning on the light and looking at his watch, he realised that he must have been asleep for a few minutes. He could hear Twelvetrees' voice down below—and Aumbrey's, he fancied. Doyle Wantage was calling to Janice, saying that Maxton was coming up the garden path and would she let him in.

The Inspector, wide-awake now, went downstairs.

He shook hands with Aumbrey, and with Twelvetrees, a tall, cadaverous man with the eyes of a Jesuit and the mouth of a bigot.

"We could have given him a lift," Aumbrey said.

"Ebor? He wouldn't have said thank-you." Twelve-trees sucked in his cheeks. "Ebor is self-sufficient. I wish I were as self-sufficient."

"One of these days he'll fall into the creek. That will test his self-sufficiency. He never learns."

Twelvetrees gave his curate a sour look. "We learn from experience. Maxton's experience seems to suggest that he can get away with it, so you may be wrong there."

"You may have to answer for all this," Doyle said. "He has sharp ears, remember."

Maxton was talking to Janice in the hall. They heard his staccato laugh, then he came in. A man just short of middle height, fortyish, dressed in a donkey-brown suit, with red-brown hair scrubbily parted on a round, forceful head.

"You're late," Doyle said. "Eight o'clock's your usual time."

"Late?" Maxton's fingers went to his wrist. "Ten minutes, that's all. Who's here, besides the skipper and his cabin-boy?"

"The skipper and his Number One," Aumbrey corrected him.

"Smith's on your right," Doyle said.

"Good. You haven't shifted any furniture around? I'm coming over to shake hands with Smith."

He did, stepping firmly, and gripping the Inspector's hand with considerable strength. "You're looking very fit, Mr. Smith."

It was said so naturally that the Inspector's mouth tightened. It was difficult to believe that those eyes were plastic discs. Maxton produced a cigarette-case.

"Janice?"

She glanced at Doyle, then took one. "Thanks, Mr. Maxton."

He flicked a lighter, and she bent forward. "Sorry!"

he said. "Running dry. . . . Ah, that's better!"

"When you've finished your party tricks," Doyle said, "there's a chair behind you."

"I'm well aware of that. Where's the machine?"

"On the window-ledge."

"Did you tape the rag-time band last night?"

"The second and third movements, yes."

"Sorry I couldn't be there. I was busy polishing up my own masterly performance. Let's see what Tennier made of it."

He walked easily to the window-recess. With no apparent difficulty he turned on the tape-recorder, ran the tape back, and started it playing.

Coming back to the chair, he lit a stubby pipe and listened attentively. At one point, Doyle Wantage crossed the room and was shifting the controls, but Maxton shook his head.

"Don't muck about with it—leave that treble alone. You're making it sound like a bloody juke-box. Straight out of the bottom of the barrel."

When the two movements had run their course, he went to the mantelpiece and propped himself against it. "Was Tennier conducting in his shirt-sleeves?"

"I seem to remember that he was," Doyle said with some caution.

"Let's hope he makes a better job of it when he's wearing his tails. You can muck around with Bernard Sholto and nobody knows the difference. Sholto himself wouldn't notice if you skipped ten bars. Or played them backwards way round. But you can't muck around with Brahms. Those horns sound like a cow in labour."

Rubbing his hands, he turned his head towards Aumbrey and Twelvetrees. "You're city types, both of you. You don't know what a cow in labour sounds like, do you? Sorry I can't think of an ecclesiastical equivalent. I may do before the night's out."

Doyle Wantage was busy with bottle and glasses. "Talking about your own masterly performance—" he began.

"Don't try to be diplomatic and head me off, Doyle. Do you expect any of the Clan tonight?"

"People drop in," Doyle said. "As you have done."

"Do you expect Turvey?"

"He's flying back from Zurich tomorrow morning. Otherwise I wouldn't expect him to absent himself."

"From your company, you mean, or your ex-wife's?"

"That's uncalled for, Ebor. What do you want to drink—whisky?"

"Please." He rubbed his hands again. They were large, stubby hands, powerful and flexible. "Is it blasphemy to take their name in vain? I don't care a damn for Turvey and I don't for Grace. What I do care about is that they're slowly but surely taking the whole pantomime out of your hands. *I'm* content to let it stay there—though surely before God if anybody's entitled to question your authority I'm that one?"

"You're less than a foot from centre-stage, Ebor," said Doyle with good humour.

Maxton gave a grunting laugh. He turned now, with unerring accuracy, to Janice Teale. The Inspector, fascinated by the man's assurance, wondered if he had memorised the initial positions of everyone in the room and plotted their subsequent movements.

"What do you think of us all, Jan? Phoneys, loonies, small-town egg-heads? You're much too well-mannered to say, so I'll tell you. There's no health in us, to quote the Prayer Book. We make music in the name of the Lord, Amen! But we've ceased to believe in the Lord. Pin Twelvetrees down and he'll quote theological sophistries. Spill three dry sherries down Aumbrey's throat and he'll babble of space-time continuums, but every one of us is a damned infidel. The big item in last year's Festival was Mass In G Minor by Doyle Wan-

tage, but Doyle has less respect for the Mass than I
have for the Establishment."

"I think I resent that," Aumbrey said dubiously.

"You *think!* My dear boy, I've every sympathy with
your lack of conviction. And everybody else's. What I
object to is this pseudo-religious label that's been stuck
on to a purely secular activity. Especially when it covers
such doubtful characters as Norris Turvey and Heneage
Iles. Not to mention Heneage's unspeakable wife, who
for so many years was your unspeakable wife, Doyle.
You know the set-up, Smith? Doyle has put you wise
to the position, Jan?"

"Speaking for myself," the Inspector said, "I know
very little about the Festival."

"Let me instruct you! Music from Bach to Sholto
dwells in the Hangar, a place so haunted by abominable
draughts and mouldy smells that you wouldn't lure a
dozen people inside if it were not a fashionable occasion. The women trail their dresses over raw concrete
and rough timber. The acoustics are of the devil. The
Artistes' Room was once a flight-crew's mess, the cloak-
rooms are canvas adjuncts, the lavatories communicate
with a cess-pit which belches back half of its contents
after heavy rain. Yet everybody comes. . . . *Why* the
hell didn't you keep things as they were?"

Twelvetrees cleared his throat. "These things get out
of hand," he said heavily.

"I know that, I know it! I'm lamenting the dead for
whom there's no resurrection. Lamenting the days
when a few people who loved music and loved what
they called their God sat together in the three front
pews of Luke and James and lifted up their hearts. Of
course it's got out of hand! That's my whole point. It
isn't the masses who've crowded the church and the
village hall until we've had to shift to the Hangar. It's
the Committee. And the Committee is packed tight
with butchers and bakers and landlords and the pro-

prieters of all the Ye Olde Trashe Shoppes."

Aumbrey pursed his lips. "Couldn't one say the same of Salzburg or Oberammergau?"

Maxton gave him the full benefit of his plastic stare. "I've no great affection for either place. But I have for Salchurch. A cult of any kind is death to art and death to sincerity, and you can quote me on that."

It was not the end of Maxton's tirade. It had subsided a little but not ceased when Doyle excused himself and followed Janice Teale into the kitchen. Before the others came, she had been cutting sandwiches and making coffee. "Would you like me to give you a hand?" he said.

"Of course not! Go back to them."

"They won't miss me. . . . I hope you're learning something from all this?"

She looked over her shoulder. "Quite a lot, but does it really matter?"

"I think it does. Maxton's right up to a point. About the way things have gradually slipped out of my hands, I mean."

"And do you mind that? At least it leaves you free to do more important things."

"I suppose that's true. . . . And if the committees and associations pulled together, I wouldn't mind. It's the private feuds that worry me."

She had a way of going unhurriedly about her own work while sparing the necessary attention for anyone who was talking to her. "So long as you don't get pulled into them, does it matter?"

"I do get pulled into them, and there's no way of avoiding it. There have always been undercurrents, but I've known which way they were pulling. Now, I'm not so sure."

The kitchen had been modernised since June; it was almost sybaritic for a household of three. She moved around it methodically, putting the coffee to settle, arranging sandwiches and cakes so that they could be taken in without fuss at the right moment.

"Does Norris Turvey worry you?" she asked suddenly.

"Why do you ask that?"

"I saw the way you threw down his letter when you'd read it this morning."

"It was so damnably smug. And this morning too I saw Laura. We're apt to forget that he has a wife. She hasn't worn well. She looks years older than her smooth, well-polished husband."

"You worry too much," she said. "About things you can't change."

She had told him that before. She had a way of ironing out his smaller worries, and he wondered if she resented the energy he wasted upon those beyond her control.

He went into his own sanctum and typed a letter. In the next room, Maxton was still talking, but the others were coming back at him and the conversation was more general. Doyle Wantage looked at the calendar on his deck. For eight more days, this would go on. After that, he would need a holiday.

The letter finished, he went upstairs and plugged in his shaver. There had been no time to freshen up since Tennier's rehearsal. A bath would have put him in better humour, but Smith, a sheep among so many wolves, shouldn't be left alone with them too long. He was hurrying back when he saw her, standing just outside the room he had left only a few minutes ago.

She had the face of a carefully-groomed Eurasian madonna, black hair parted to show a line of scalp above a wide, high forehead. "We let ourselves in," she said. "You don't mind?"

He came more slowly down the lower half-dozen stairs. "I don't mind at all. You gave me a surprise, Grace."

"A pleasant one?"

She was a trifle dated, he thought. Her lipstick was too red, her hands too claw-like. "Where's Heneage?" he asked.

"Talking to Ebor and your other guests." She looked around, patronisingly. "It seems a long time since I was here."

"Three or four months, yes."

"I drove past a few weeks ago, but you were sitting in the garden with a precocious-looking infant."

"Nina? She isn't at all precocious. I detest precocious children almost as much as I detest clever women."

"That's quite good, at such short notice. I *did* want to see you, though. And talk to you."

"You're talking to me now."

"Until someone opens a door, yes."

He passed her and turned on the light in his room. "Is this better?"

She came in slowly and sat down. He remained standing, ramrod-straight beside the door.

"Doyle," she said, "when is all this ridiculous business going to stop?"

He pushed his hands into his pockets. It was a bad sign that she remembered well.

"I'm not aware of being involved in any business, ridiculous or otherwise."

"I'm talking about the girl."

"I thought you were leading up to that. What has it to do with you?"

"You're public property. You belong to the community. You're worth a ninepenny rate. . . ."

"I would have put it rather higher than that. Even so, what connection is there between my rateable value and my domestic affairs?"

The madonna-like face contorted viciously. "I never knew an intelligent man who could be so stupid when he chose. Do you mind if I help myself to a drink, even though this isn't my house now?"

"Do by all means."

There was whisky on the table, though Doyle rarely touched it when he was working. "Are these glasses clean?" she asked "Sorry, I shouldn't have said that. I'm sure your housekeeper takes good care of all that."

"She does."

"I had a reporter to see me today, Doyle. He's tried several times to see you. Dermott Casey of the *Daily Empire*. He thinks their readership may be interested to know that Doyle Wantage, one of British music's most colourful personalities, has taken a young and exceedingly attractive girl into his house—"

"You can tell your journalist friend that I'll watch every word he writes, and sue for libel if he oversteps the facts by a single comma. Is that clear?"

"Quite clear. But you won't shut up village gossip as easily as that."

"What is it saying?"

"That this girl is living here with you as your wife and that the child is yours. What else do you expect them to say?"

He pulled in a long, deep breath.

"Grace, you were always a bitch. Perhaps one shouldn't remind you that I was petitioner and Heneage co-respondent at the time of our divorce. Perhaps one shouldn't mention your association with Norris Turvey now. You're the last person to talk about my morals."

She purred with satisfaction, Usually, he was more difficult to rouse.

"Darling, your morals don't interest me. From personal experience, I wouldn't have thought you oversexed. But if advancing years are developing that side of your nature and you can't do without it, for God's sake put her somewhere in a cottage off the main road and enjoy her behind drawn curtains. Don't parade her in front of Salchurch."

"Or in front of you—isn't that what you mean?"

"Doyle, I don't care a damn!"

"I think you do. Why should it bother you that your ex-husband happens to have found someone who cares whether he lives or dies?"

"One is naturally interested in the health of one's employer," she retorted. "Unless she's a disciple?"

"No, I pay her. But not for what you imagine."

The smile she gave him was a slow, contemptuous curling of her full red lips. "I could almost believe you, Doyle. Your idealism's almost offensive. But I should be alone. There isn't a soul in this village who doesn't believe you're sleeping with this girl."

"Then any further protest seems pointless, doesn't it?"

"Quite pointless! And there are things I *know*, Doyle. Things you would perhaps like to know. . . ."

"Is this a return to the sort of nerve-war we enjoyed in the happy days of our marriage?"

"If you like to think of it that way. But apart from what I know, it wouldn't be good policy to antagonise me, would it? After all, I do still have some influence over Heneage. And Heneage virtually backs the show, doesn't he?"

His head was on one side. He could hear Janice moving about in the kitchen. It helped to know that she was there.

"So we play it as dirty as that!" he said. "Listen, if Heneage withdraws his support, that's a matter for the Finance Committee. I've been told that often enough about other matters. You'll have the pleasure of telling the Committee that I won't sack my housekeeper and so you've influenced your husband to put the screw on."

"It hasn't come to that—yet."

"But it's a threat held over my head at a time when I need a reasonably easy mind. We'd better join your dear husband, Grace, before I lose my temper. That poker in the hearth—it's a bit too conveniently placed."

She rose lazily from the chair. "Banked fires!" she said. "I believe that in certain circumstances you *could* kill, you know."

"In certain circumstances, who couldn't?"

Ebor Maxton had sat down and taken his place with the others. It was Heneage Iles who stood now, nervously fingering his glass. He was a slim, Byronically handsome man with an affectation of elegance. In his relationship with Grace, he reminded Doyle of a fox who has seized a prize hen and been discovered while gorging himself by the farmhouse dog. His eyes fastened like claws on Grace as she came into the room.

"So you've had your little private talk?" he asked. "What was it about this time, Doyle—music or money?"

"Neither," Doyle said, sitting down next to Inspector Smith. "We talked about murder."

"Whose?" Heneage asked querulously.

"We hadn't got around to that. We talked about it academically, we discussed its ethics."

It surprised him that he could be reasonably inventive verbally as well as musically. "I wonder," he went on, "if one is ever justified—"

Heneage Iles' eyes were unnaturally dark in his pale face. "I wonder!" he said.

"Never in any circumstances!" Twelvetrees said with emphasis.

"Not in *any?*" Doyle was looking at Heneage. "Where exactly does murder become manslaughter and tail off into justifiable homicide?"

"A jury is often called upon to decide that question," Inspector Smith said.

"Give me a drink, Heneage," Grace said in a flat voice.

He brought it. "Curious subject, murder. Actually, Doyle, I thought Grace wanted to talk to you about the seating accommodation."

Doyle felt suddenly tired of it all. Ebor Maxton's pronouncements he could stand, but not much more of this. "We settled the seating," he said, "then went on to more important things."

For once, Maxton eased the tension. "Now we're all here, could we run that tape through again?"

By the time the Brahms had been played, and Tennier discussed, and Janice's sandwiches eaten, and everyone had drunk to the success of tomorrow's enterprise, murder had receded into the background and Heneage Iles was talking unsteadily about making an early night of it.

"I suppose we'll all be together again tomorrow night?" He looked vaguely at Grace. "Why shouldn't everybody come along to our place?"

"It's a bit late to change round," Doyle said. "People seem to drift here. It's grown to be a habit."

"It was an idea, that's all. How are you getting home, Maxton? Give you a lift?"

"I like walking," Ebor Maxton said.

He waited till they had gone, then went for his own coat. "May as well let them start their nightly row now as after they've dropped me in Salchurch. Goodnight, everybody." He put his head round the kitchen door. "That includes you, Jan."

"Goodnight, Mr. Maxton." She came into the hall. "Do be careful, won't you? Go round by the road to-night."

"Why? Midnight and high noon are alike to me. *The dark is light enough.*"

Doyle took him to the garden gate, then came back to the kitchen.

"Surely you've nothing more to do?"

"Not tonight. I've just stacked away the dishes."

"Come in and have a last drink with us. The hard core of our company."

Those few minutes, at the ending of the day, restored his good humour. Smith in his newly-cleaned and pressed suit, thoughtful by the fire, and the girl with her quiet voice and softly shining hair.

"We talk so much about music in this house," he said, "and so seldom listen to it. Music's becoming an article of commerce. I feel like going into the wilderness."

"You thought you were doing that when you came here," Smith reminded him.

"I'll go back to the Camargue." He looked at Janice. "Do you think your adopted daughter would appreciate the Camargue?"

"She'd love the gipsies and the flamingoes. But you wouldn't go back. You couldn't."

"But you'd go with me if I did?"

"I'd give it careful consideration," she said, and he laughed.

But later, in his bedroom, he was thinking of Grace. It was easy to dismiss what she had said, but less easy to forget it.

He opened the window and stood with his hands on the sill. The night was clear and calm. Far across the marsh, the lighthouse flashed—once, twice, three times. He remembered other nights when he had watched the circling beam. Sleepless nights. . . . And he looked over his shoulder at the bed with sudden distaste.

5

Arts and Craft

Ebor Maxton walked with head erect and slightly on one side. He knew where he was to a yard by the ring of the unsurfaced road, the complexity of echoes from wall and hedge. Half a mile from the nearest Salchurch houses, he turned through a wicket-gate on to the riverside path, never slackening his pace, never relaxing that sensory vigilance which is the salvation of the blind.

There were places where the path ran within inches of the river, others where it meandered among a fringe of trees, but it was never far from the sluggish, silent water. It was very cold. Here at the edge of the marsh, frost whitened the grass a month earlier than anywhere else in the neighbourhood.

Cutting off the road's long detour, the path rejoined it at the foot of the village street, where the creek passed under a bridge. He climbed a few stone steps and leaned against the bridge-parapet. Luke and James chimed the half-hour. He crossed the street and pushed open a gate. The garden smelt of wet leaves, of early autumn chrysanthemums and wood-smoke. The Turveys had a gardener. He crossed the lawn to a side-door and gently tapped. After a few moments it was opened and he went in, waiting till he heard it closed again.

"Laura?" he said.

"I'm here."

"I know you're there. I wanted the pleasure of speaking your name."

"I thought you would have gone home long ago. It's so late."

"I'm on my way there now. But don't chuck me out, Laura. Let me sit down for ten minutes."

"Come in. . . . Careful, there's a stool—"

"I-spy, with my non-existent eye—My radar's working well tonight. When is Norris the Devil coming home?"

"Tomorrow morning."

"Zurich little knows the favour it's doing me. Laura, I've been drinking. Give me some coffee."

He sat down and waited till she came back and gave him the cup.

"It's nice to see you sitting there, Laura. You're looking very pretty tonight. I like that dress."

He leaned forward, smoothing it with his powerful fingers. "It's a nice colour. It suits you. . . . There, shall I go on jumping through hoops and showing you how clever I am?"

"Please don't." She put both her hands on his. "It isn't necessary with me."

"Then I won't. I won't even throw off the casual remark that brown is B flat minor to me, and I do love that one. Most people think it's so damned original."

"Where have you been drinking tonight?"

"At Wantage's place. These pre-Festival get-togethers used to have some significance, but not any more. . . . The night before the show, the first night of the show, the last night—we still do it, but it's all washed up. It's got to be a habit."

"Who was there?"

"Twelvetrees and the Cabin Boy. Aumbrey, to save your asking. Grace Iles and Heneage. And a policeman from Penrhuan, old crony of Wantage's younger days. Retiring type, fatherly voice, but I wouldn't care to get on the wrong side of him professionally if I'd just murdered my worst friend. And the Teale girl—the *jeune personne* Doyle recently installed as his housekeeper. I've been holding forth on music, commercial exploitation, and artistic integrity like the cocky bastard I am. But it was called for. . . . Yes, dammit."

"Will you be doing anything, apart from the recitals?"

"I don't want anything more. There's no organ in the Hangar, so God be thanked I won't be called upon to reinforce Elgar. Bach, Franck, Widor—they'll bring in the cream. Tennier can have the skim-milk. They can't commercialise *me*, though I know they'd like to put a banner across the Luke and James chancel saying that my recital's sponsored by the Shilstone Brewery Company."

"Do you have to make a joke of everything, Ebor? A bitter joke? I hate to think you're ever sorry for yourself."

"Sometimes you put your finger on the spot," he said.

He sat in silence, groping for some tangible image of her. She had married Turvey when she was nineteen. That was before he started moving up in the world. He was working then for a construction company in Bolton, and Laura was a typist in the general office. Since then he had prospered, grown plump with good living and smooth with social rubbings. She never had. Her accent had scarcely altered. She had remained the same. . . .

"Yesterday, today, and for ever!" he murmured.

"What was that?"

"Nothing, nothing. . . . Laura, I'm tired tonight and I can't think why."

"You should give up the church or the school. Or the Festival."

"And thereby save a third of my time. What would I do with it?"

"Rest, take things easy."

"I can do that through all eternity. . . . Laura, if ever you can take your light from under the bushel, whatever a bushel is, I'd like you to meet Smith. I've been talking to him tonight about something I usually avoid. . . . The limited experience of a man born blind."

"I've sometimes wondered about that," she said. "But it isn't a thing—"

"—one cares to talk about," he finished for her. "Though I'm not sensitive or embarrassed about it. Not at all. Still, it's interesting. If I were stone-deaf, I could understand a scientific explanation of sound, but I still wouldn't know what the experience of hearing means. So does that lack of experience affect character and judgement?"

Her hands moved away from his. "I don't understand you, Ebor."

"The facts!" he said. "You have to have all the facts. A sightless man never has."

He went through the cigarette ritual again. "Which variation this time? Running dry? Or shall I say it needs a new flint? I'll show you some day how it's done. Very simple. . . . The end-product of all this elaborate build-up, Laura, is that I wish I could see you."

"You know me. . . ."

"Yes. That ties up with what I was saying a moment ago, but it doesn't matter." He steadied his thoughts, and his voice. "Has it been too bad this week?"

"Not too bad. He's been away since Tuesday."

"Have you done any work—serious work?"

"No. It seems a waste of time."

"Why? I could flatter you and talk about the need for self-expression, but that wouldn't help much. Still, I hope you'll keep it up."

"I shall. Three hours every day."

"It'll keep your fingers warm, if nothing else. I often think about that first morning. I wondered who the devil you were. Please would I teach you to play the piano. I remember asking *why*, and you gave me some nonsense about hating the idea of looking at a closed door and wishing you could open it and doing nothing about it. God, I didn't know what I was letting myself in for."

"I wonder why I really came?"

He slapped his knee. "You wanted to keep up with the Joneses. Your Jones of a husband with his half-dozen pat platitudes. The Jones bitch who tormented the life out of Wantage for years and then married Heneage Iles. All the Joneses in this lousy little snob's paradise. Salchurch will be full of 'em tomorrow. Prattling about atonality, worshipping the incomprehensible and spitting on simplicity. They'd have Mozart looking after the car-park and touching his cap to clots like your husband if he were alive in Salchurch today."

He felt along the table-edge for his cup. "I'll tell you! No I won't . . . Yes, by God I will!"

"Tell me what?"

"Norris said to me next day that he'd heard his wife had developed an interest in music. Said it was a damn good thing. You'd never had the chance when you were young, and unfortunately you were not the type to adapt yourself to a changed environment. I said what the hell did he mean by that, and it got him a bit flustered. We were in the Bull and Boar, you understand, with the deputy-assistant mayor-elect of Shilstone on one side and the clerk to the magistrates' clerk's clerk on the other. So Norris raised his voice three notches and started jabbering about the importance of integrating artistic values with the rapidly-changing exigencies of the times."

He thought she would laugh at that, but her voice was low and serious. "I haven't moved up with Norris."

"Thank God for that!"

He lay back in the chair. "Laura, you've given me a sense of purpose."

"And you've given me happiness. Purpose? I don't know about that."

"Odd, isn't it! You give me purpose, I give you happiness, and then I leave you, and you wait here for your lord and master to come home and exercise his conjugal rights."

"Do you have to remind me?"

"I'm merely quoting again. He once told me that when he expected to be late home he instructed you to stay awake until he arrived. I fell into the trap and asked why. And he told me. . . . I wish I'd Doyle Wantage's integrity or Smith's philosophy or your ability to endure. But I lack the lot."

He listened as she moved about the room. "You'll be at the grand opening tomorrow?" he asked.

"I don't think so. Sunday is more important to me. I can sit in the south aisle and watch."

"Come and rescue me afterwards if you can think of a plausible excuse. No one can throw stones at us in Luke and James. . . . By the way, is Norris on his travels again next week or do we have to endure him till the end of the Festival?"

"He has an appointment in Glasgow on Tuesday. Can you see me then?"

"Then or any other day."

"I thought we might go into Shilstone or Penrhuan."

"Splendid! Though I don't remember such a suggestion coming from you before."

"I've some shopping to do. And one or two calls to make. We'd have a few hours together. I could come round for you."

"About one," he suggested. "I've a period on Tuesday morning, latish. . . . Sure there's nothing wrong, no special reason behind it?"

"No special reason," she said, but his instincts told him that she was being unusually evasive. Still, why quibble? It was something to look forward to.

"Three more days, then. You can drop me at the Library. I'd like to check a stack of new Brailles they've got in for me."

He got up, put out his hands. "I have carnal lusts like any men, Laura, though I sometimes waste my time trying to refine them. Give me a moment. I want to take home the smell of your hair and the taste of your mouth, and the hell with Norris."

It was well past midnight when he made his way through a village deserted and silent but for the hollow call of owls in the churchyard elms. There was no hurry; he took his time. Parvings, his place in a corner of the school grounds, was a small converted farm, its lands absorbed into the playing-fields. His sister kept house for him—a convenient arrangement as she taught English and History at the school.

She had waited up. Ebor Maxton was in awe of nobody, but his sister came nearer to inspiring awe in him than any person he knew. Steered by unfailing instinct, he went straight to his chair between window and fireplace.

"Where have you been?" she asked.

"Out."

"I asked *where*."

"You'd have made a damn good orphanage matron, Ruth. I've been to see Doyle Wantage and his weekend guests. Since then I've been talking to Laura Turvey and drinking her coffee."

"You're a bigger fool than I took you for."

She was a dark, angular woman with a singularly baleful stare which, perhaps fortunately, was lost upon her brother.

"You're a nark, Ruth. In your jaundiced eyes any man who follows his own inclinations is either a fool or a knave. I never pretended to be dedicated."

"Was Norris there?"

"You know quite well that if Norris had been there I shouldn't have called."

She drew a low stool opposite his chair. "Ebor, what good can possibly come of it?"

"I expect nothing, because I believe more in the malice of fate than the goodness of providence. But one great good could come of it. . . . Her release from a man who isn't fit to lick her muddiest pair of shoes."

"You call that good?"

"I would, if it happened."

"She may not wish to be released."

Her voice was tinged with malice. "Norris Turvey happens to be a rich man. Women will put up with a great deal for security and comfort. Have you considered that?"

"Qualify those terms!" he said. "Qualify them and I'll consider them. To you, comfort and security mean money in the bank. But there are other kinds of comfort. The heart needs to be comfortable, the soul needs to be secure."

"I only hope," she retorted, "that you confine your attentions to her heart and soul. Norris might need a lot of convincing that you do. You're fooling yourself, Ebor! You must be mad if you think for one moment—"

"That she'd marry me if she could? Don't you think she would?"

"Frankly, I don't."

"Why not? Apart from lacking your useful fifth sense, I'm reasonably normal. Wouldn't you think so? And unlike you, I'm not a born celibate."

"Celibates are not born," she said. "They're made."

"You know, you may have something there. . . . I've often wondered why you revel so unconvincingly in your virginity."

She bit back an angry retort. "Have you had supper? That's why I stayed up, not to argue with you."

"I've had sandwiches, coffee, whisky, and more coffee. It's whisky's turn again. Is there any left? Wait—I'll see. You might lie to me." He went to the sideboard. "Getting low. Will you join me?"

"No."

"You might remember your manners."

"Ebor, you're a perpetual enigma to me."

"What of it? I am to myself. But don't tie up Laura with that. The trouble is that like most other people in this village and the Turvey family in particular, you're a lousy snob."

He came back to the chair, holding the bottle by its neck. "If Laura were the local doctor's daughter instead of the fifth child of a Bolton brewers' delivery man you'd be less worried about moral issues."

"You don't like the Turveys, do you?"

"I don't like any breed of jackals. Not even human ones."

"They're realistic. You're not."

"Realistic enough to sell out a three-truck haulage business and use the cash to finance the bright boy of the family. Norris. Brains and acquisitive instincts. Public utilities. He's acquired a veneer. Laura hasn't. She says bath instead of bahth. That's fatal. To hold your own socially in the sweet south you mustn't wear red roses or white, but the green carnations of the stockbroker belt."

"How ably you defend her!" Ruth said bitingly.

"And how badly she needs it! Norris isn't satisfied with ten thousand a year and a directorship or two. He's got one eye on Westminster. Laura wouldn't be much good to him there, would she?"

"Has Norris told you she wouldn't?"

"His brother has. His father has. They're proud of him, remember. He's probably the only Turvey to pay supertax. If only he'd married a different woman, how far he might have gone! How important it is—don't you agree, Mr. Maxton—for a rising man to have an educated wife."

Sensing Ruth's uneasiness, he emptied what was left of the whisky and took an angry swig. "I suppose you're exaggerating as usual," Ruth said.

"I never exaggerate. Under-statement's my forte. Mrs. Turvey senior is a pillar of the Mothers' Union. She has the bug. She sent her small grand-daughter to me for lessons."

"Isabel?"

"Yes. Norris's niece. Was she getting on nicely, asks Mrs. Turvey senior, and I said *well* . . . Did I think elocution lessons would help her, and I said *well* again . . . Didn't I think she was quite a clever child, and I said no, I didn't."

"You never knew the meaning of tact, Ebor."

"You mean I'm not a habitual bloody liar. I'm willing to exercise tact if it's in a good cause. That wasn't. I told her Isabel's a nice, pleasant, lovable child, and she says that won't take her very far, will it? I exploded then and said *Christ*. She thought it was blasphemy, but it was an appeal for help."

"This was in church?"

"In Luke and James, yes. I thought I might do Laura a bit of good on the side, but it didn't come off. I said look at Laura—she wasn't so brilliant, but you'd have to go a long way before you found anybody with the same charm and sincerity. She said well yes of course! But such people did give themselves away, didn't they? Lack of education *was* a terrible handicap to themselves and others, wasn't it?"

He flexed his fingers till they cracked. "You see what I mean? What's illicit—their contempt for her or my regard?"

"It's a good attempt at self-justification, Ebor. Where is Norris tonight?"

"Switzerland. Tomorrow he returns to shed the light of his countenance upon us and the Festival."

"And how many people will tell him that you've been calling on Laura in his absence?"

"At least twenty. The same twenty who tell me that he sleeps with Grace when Heneage is in London." He up-ended the bottle with a regretful grimace. "One man stands aloof from all this nonsense, Ruth. Doyle Wantage. He needs neither power nor wealth to justify his existence. There's a thing called integrity. . . . That never appealed to Grace. She didn't understand what integrity means. So she left him for Heneage, who was born to power. Three thousand acres spells power even in these days. But now she's discarding him. It's Grace and Norris. Two people like that either clash or merge. They're merging." .

He got up and made for the inner door. "Fusion!" he said. "I read somewhere that in the sub-microscopic world of atomic suns and galaxies, sparks of radiation are released when fusion occurs. And they do the damage. Watch out for sparks."

Ebor slept late next morning. His Saturday lunch-hour schedule usually included a pint at the Bull and Boar. The village was *en fête*.

Bernard Sholto, whose new work would be performed on Thursday next, was also in the Bull and Boar with two music-critics and a scion of minor royalty.

Twelvetrees was in Luke and James, querulously reminding himself that he was a man of God, yet anxiously assessing possible financial returns.

Doyle Wantage was still in bed. Tennier sat in his private room at the Riverside Hotel, frowning over some obscure bowing. While that evening's audience disported itself between the various pubs, snack-counters, and Ye Olde Cafés, where prices varied according to the number of spindles on their fumed-oak chairs.

Inspector Smith had left Bargehouse Mill after a late breakfast and walked to the outskirts of Salchurch. He leaned against a wind-bleached gate, viewing the scene from a safe distance. It was pleasant to feel detached.

He was as conscious as anyone else of the Salchurch undercurrents, but they were no concern of his. And for that he was mildly grateful. Lunch at one-thirty, a private introduction to the Hangar by Doyle Wantage, and then the evening concert—it was a pleasant prospect.

A line of brick chimneys and serrated house-roofs marked the main street. Beyond them soared the tower of Luke and James. He could see Marsh School, the ancient edifice where Ebor Maxton and his sister taught. The only intrusive note was provided by the Hangar itself, an unlovely structure fringed this morning by a number of sadly-droopings flags.

Continuing his walk, he came to the school playing-fields, and wondered if Maxton lived nearby and might be at home. A number of boys were strenuously amusing themselves on the turf, and one of them directed the Inspector towards Parvings. A narrow gate was set in the hedge, and over it he saw Maxton, hatless and shirt-sleeved, tying up chrysanthemums. Smith watched for a minute or so, admiring his uncanny dexterity, then entered the garden.

"So you've dug me out!" Maxton said genially. "Taking a stroll before the ordeal?" He laughed loudly. "I heard your cough a hundred yards away." Then, standing back from the mass of blooms, "Pretty good show, don't you think?"

"Very good indeed. I have some fine ones at Penrhuan. The big shaggy things that seem out of fashion these days."

Maxton nodded. "Lot of trouble—disbudding and keeping the filth off. But they make a nice splash of colour on this side of the house."

Smith listened to the shouts from over the hedge. "You don't have lessons on Saturday morning?"

"Usually we do. Have to keep the little devils' minds off sex and sadism. But Festival Saturday's always a bit chancey. Nothing's organised. A lot of parents will be along and half the boys on leave. Ruth's in school now— my sister. She's the dedicated one, not me. Care for a drink?"

The Inspector followed him indoors. "What'll you have—Scotch, gin, sherry?"

"A little sherry. Spirits don't agree with me."

"They don't with me, but I drink 'em. . . . Which reminds me, the whisky's gone. Drank the last drop last night."

Smith sat down, taking stock of the room and its pleasant view across the fields. Ebor refused to sample his tobacco, but lit a cigarette. "Doyle on edge?" he asked. "He usually is on the first day."

"I haven't seen him this morning."

"What d'you think of the girl, Smith?"

"I was here in June when she applied for the job."

"There's a cagey answer for you! Kindly but full of reservations."

"No, I'm not making reservations at all. I liked her then and I like her now. But I was surprised by the change in her. I wouldn't have taken her for the same person."

"Shows what a few months in civilised company does for you. She hasn't a clue where Doyle's work is concerned—you'll have gathered that. Couldn't tell a crotchet from a bull's foot. And yet she holds her own. Defends herself against all comers by saying she doesn't know, then makes some remark of astonishing perspicacity. Certainly a pleasant change from Grace. Lustful bitch, Grace. And Doyle's one of those rare characters who believe that love and sex should dwell together. Hence the split."

He helped himself to another finger of gin. "More sherry, Smith? No? I'd like to have your unvarnished opinion of us all. Lot of old women, eh? In my case it's excusable. When you hear all and see nothing you get an odd slant on life. Anyway, I hope Doyle marries the girl and she's strong-willed enough to throw Grace out of the house next time she calls."

He slapped back the cork into the gin-bottle. "Would you like to walk over with me to Luke and James? I'd like to run through tomorrow's programme before the herd starts prowling around."

They left the house and went towards the church. The Festival could scarcely have enjoyed better weather for its opening day. It was almost windless, the leaves just turning colour, the sky's pale blue fading to a golden haze on the horizon. Smith paused at the churchyard gate, his eyes moving along the many-windowed nave, then upward to the tower, a soaring period to the chapter of magnificence below.

They entered by the West Door and made their way to the chancel. The vast spaces were light and airy; no dark forest of woodwork cluttered the floor. Row upon row of plain oak chairs stood between wide strips of rush matting. Maxton threaded his way through them with no hesitation, unlocked the console, and waved a proud hand.

The Inspector was remembering Aumbrey's story. Maxton's protests could have been true. The organ in its severely functional case was high above the chancel and a long way from the console. Turvey's cry of alarm *could* have been unheard. And yet . . .

A ray of sunlight burnished Maxton's red-brown hair. The Inspector drew back into the shadows, listening and watching. It was an experience he would not easily forget. Sunlight splintered and fused again by the painted glass, pools of colour on the grey floor, and the river of sound that flowed so nobly through those cavernous spaces—perhaps, he thought, a mere policeman should kneel.

It was some time before he realised that they were not alone. A woman had come into the church and was standing across the chancel, her eyes on Maxton. A woman in her thirties, he judged, slender and composed. Her face could have been beautiful once, now it was shadowed, hollowed. . . . Though as the light caught her, rapt and motionless, there was some beauty left.

She smiled and came nearer, and still nearer till she was close beside the console. Then the Inspector inadvertently moved, and a prayer-book fell to the floor. She turned and their eyes met, she remained frozenly still as Maxton lifted his hands and flicked back the stops.

"You're there, Smith?"

"Yes, I'm here." His eyes were still on the woman.

"Franck wrote for those brilliant reeds you usually find in French organs." His feet passed swiftly up and down the pedalboard and a shattering fanfare of trumpets sounded from above the chancel. "He would have appreciated these."

The woman slowly walked away. Smith followed her to the door, where she turned and faced him.

"Thank you," she said. "I didn't expect you to understand."

"I didn't," he admitted. Her words had the round, open vowel-sounds of the distant north.

"I often come in when Mr. Maxton is playing. But he doesn't like people to listen, so I never tell him."

"Neither will I."

He watched her go down the flagged walk to the gate. A trivial incident, but one that had moved him in some inexplicable way. He turned back to the chancel.

"I heard voices," Maxton said.

"Your hearing must be very acute."

"It is. She often comes in. She stands there, she never speaks, she goes out so quietly. Laura—Turvey's wife. She's a very quiet person."

His fingers moved to the Choir stops. Inspector Smith instinctively straightened his back and drew his shoulders together—his professional stance. For it suddenly came to him that all this might, after all, become a professional matter.

Since hearing Aumbrey's story, he had come full-circle. One small sound against the monumental silence of the great church came to his ears, so high as to be scarcely audible. Its pitch seemed to vary, as a closely-observed star seems to shift and waver under the arch of space, but that was an illusion. The sound persisted; piercing, fading, piercing again.

There was a slight smile on Maxton's face. A single key was depressed under the third finger of his right hand. And the stop he had drawn, Smith noticed, was *lieblich piccolo*.

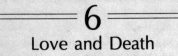

6

Love and Death

Inspector Smith left Bargehouse Mill with Doyle soon after half past two.

"Turvey's back from Zurich," Doyle said. "I didn't mention it while we were in the house because Jan worries about my involvements. He'll be at the Hangar this afternoon. On the credit side, you may also see Tennier at work. He's almost certain to run through the Brahms again. The Mozart too, if Colin Radwell arrives on time."

He was nervous this afternoon, driving badly, wondering if Tennier would be in one of his bad moods, if the orchestra would let Radwell down in the concerto's last glittering movement.

"I'll efface myself as much as possible," Smith said.

"No. I'll be glad to have you at my elbow. So long as you're not bored. . . ."

At first sight, the Hangar's interior was vastly depressing. At considerable cost, it had been decorated with more or less taste. The seating was adequate, including a monstrous tier above the arena, and a reasonably efficient heating-system had been installed. Yet the overall effect was too sombre for a joyful occasion.

There were no more than a dozen people in sight when they entered. Sounds of hammering echoed through the empty gloom. A man was arranging gilt chairs on the platform. The piano was shrouded in a dust-sheet, the conductor's rostrum had a rail missing, and on his desk lay a gaily-coloured weekly magazine.

Doyle carried a bag in which Janice had carefully packed his evening clothes. He would not come into his own till next week, but still, he would be much in the public eye tonight. They crossed the platform. A door at the end of a corridor bore a paper label—*Mr. Wantage.* Doyle opened it. A little man carrying three nested chairs brushed past.

"Mr. Turvey's somewhere around, Mr. Wantage. Been asking for you. Said he'd hang around. Must have been in the Boar since opening-time. Can't walk straight. God, is he high!"

"Let's hope he's too high to bother looking for me any more," Doyle said.

The room was austerely plain. Two chairs, a table stacked high with music, a bowl-fire on a low shelf, and beside it a pair of evening shoes and a cracked mirror. An unshaded bulb provided harsh illumination.

"Make yourself comfortable if that's possible." Doyle put down his bag. "If I'm nowhere around at five or so, go into the village and have a meal. I'll want nothing more to eat till we get home later, but you may."

"I doubt that." The Inspector picked up some sheets of manuscript from the table. "So this is what we shall hear on Tuesday! I wish it conveyed something to me. *Tantae molis erat.* . . . That conveys just as little, I'm afraid."

"So great a labour. . . . The fruit of much thought, much work. It was started years ago and finished soon after your visit in June, just in time for rehearsals. That may suggest a train of thought. . . ."

"It does." The Inspector nodded. "A pleasant train."

"And on Tuesday it goes out from me. Procreation, birth—then what? In a curious way, there's a sense of loss when you hear something performed that has been locked for so long in your own heart and mind."

"I shall be thinking of that on Tuesday. And listening without much understanding but with considerable pride."

Doyle Wantage's face lit with one of his rare, illuminating smiles. "I appreciate that."

And as he said it, there came a loud rap on the door.

Doyle grimaced. "So soon?"

"It may not be."

"I think it is. There's a drunken self-assurance about that knock."

He pulled open the door. "I'm right, you're wrong. . . . No, I'm not talking to you, Norris. I rather thought you'd find me."

"And rather hoped I wouldn't, eh?"

He had a thick voice, plummy, slurred. There was an easy smile on his face as he came into the room. A dark, good-looking man in a heavy way, fluid in his movements, eyes flickering like a snake's tongue. Lips too thick, too moist. He raised one eyebrow at the Inspector.

"Friend?"

"This is Norris Turvey," Doyle said to Smith.

"Glad to meet you," Turvey said, the smile fixed, the eyes still flickering.

"I'm very busy, Norris," said Doyle.

"I've never wasted your time yet. Yours or anybody else's. I'm a busy man myself. Time's money."

"I heard you were back." Doyle switched on the bowl-fire, for there in the subterranean depths of the Hangar the air was chill. "Sorry you couldn't be with us last night."

"I was busy last night. Long way from home and beauty last night." He looked disparagingly at Smith. "I'm one of the world's workers. Like the boss said to the office-boy, work eight hours a day and don't worry and then they'll make you a director and you'll work eighteen and have all the bloody worry. That's what I have. *All* the bloody worry. Milk-run from Zurich, Piper to Exeter, eighty em pee aitch from there and home before the pubs were open."

Doyle sat down. "You enjoy it, Norris."

"I enjoy everything. Take life as it comes."

The odour of second-hand spirits enveloped the Inspector, who coughed slightly but made no comment.

"Everything seems to be under control," Doyle said. "The usual routine. Your turn will come when it's all over. General post-mortem meeting on Monday week."

"Meaning that I'm redundant at the moment and I can get the hell out of it! Is that it?"

"Not at all."

"Did old Barclay tell you just now that I was looking for you? Did he tell you I was drunk?"

"He didn't use that precise term."

"Well, I am. . . . Bloody drunk."

"You could always carry a good load, Norris."

Smith was looking steadily from one man to the other. Doyle Wantage, rake-thin, a bundle of nerves. Turvey smooth and sleek in spite of his condition, well-fed, an extrovert if ever there was one. Turvey took a short black cheroot from a leather case and lit it.

"Wantage, I've allowed myself a little—stimulus because I want to talk to you. Privately. I've been promising myself for weeks that I'd have a talk with you one of these days. Privately. I've said to myself, I'm going to knock hell out of Wantage at 3:30 P.M. on the opening day of the Wantage Festival. Because that's what it is— the Wantage Festival. So it's 3:30. And I'm going to knock hell out of you. *Privately.*"

Smith said, coldly, "Shall I call the police?"

Doyle's mouth twitched. "I don't think it's necessary."

"Police?" repeated Turvey. *"Call the police?* And who the hell do you think you are?"

"A witness you'll find difficult to intimidate," Smith said.

"We'd better hear what's on his mind," Doyle said.

"No—I'd like you to stay." Smith had got up, but Doyle motioned him back to the chair. "As a favour to me, unless you'd rather remain aloof from it all?"

"As you wish."

Smith took out his pouch and began the ritual that never failed to steady his nerves. Norris Turvey swayed on his feet. He went to the washbowl and lifted a handful of water to his face. It seemed to steady him, but Doyle cut in before he could speak.

"You probably know, Smith, that for some time past there's been a curious three-sided relationship between my ex-wife Grace, her husband, and Turvey. It has nothing whatever to do with me, but for some reason I seem to be the meeting-point for all their animosities."

Turvey's head went higher. He put one finger in his collar and pursed his lips, a preening gesture. He said more coherently, "I don't want to talk about your ex-wife. I want to talk about your present housekeeper."

Doyle's facial muscles tightened. He splayed his right hand on the table then slowly relaxed it. "What about my housekeeper?"

"Say I've got your welfare at heart. Prominent local resident. Pillar of the community. I don't want to see you taken for a ride."

"Coming from you—" Doyle began, then shrugged his shoulders. "What makes you suggest that I might be?"

"Interested, eh? Wouldn't like it now if I walked out without satisfying your curiosity, would you?"

"Norris, it's the busiest day of the year for me. I can spare you five minutes, that's all."

"You'll spare me just as long as I want." He wagged his finger. "And if your friend doesn't like what he hears, don't blame me. I said *privately.*"

"You're wasting time, Norris."

"You've never been self-sufficient. You like to lean, Doyle. Not the way some men do. . . . But you've got to have a stimulus. Grace says that. What's more, you can fool yourself. Kid yourself about the stimulus even if it's phoney. Grace says that too. You've been doing that. I'm talking about Jan. You took her in. You'll have been knocking her off every night and twice on Sundays and you feel good. But it doesn't fool me, the little set-up you have at Bargehouse. You're talking to a character who knows her and did quite a bit of knocking-off himself."

Doyle fumbled in a box on the table and lit a cigarette. The paper stuck to his lip; a spot of blood showed where he pulled it away.

"I get around, Doyle. I've a lot of interests in life. I move in circles you wouldn't know. Why not? I married Laura before I started climbing. She hasn't climbed. She's not built that way. So I get around. Doesn't do her any harm, does me a lot of good. That's how I ran across Jan. She gets around too. Or did in those days."

He flicked ash from the cheroot over the manuscript sheets. "Didn't you make enquiries? Didn't you ask for references? After all, you've some nice bits of old silver at Bargehouse."

"I like to accept people on their face value." Doyle was keeping his voice steady. He glanced at Smith, who sat in the corner with finger-tips judicially pressed together. Turvey roared with laughter and clapped Doyle on the back.

"Face value! I like that! Oh yes, I do care for that! I used to be the same. Trusting. Not now! Listen, I'll tell you a thing or two. . . ."

Doyle got stiffly to his feet. "You'd better get out, Norris."

"I said, take it *easy*. You don't know yourself, Doyle. She came up from Bristol way to London five long years ago. Respectable family. I've heard her talk about her old mother and a sister or two. There are easy ways for a girl like that to make money. She found them. Matter of fact, she got plenty out of me. That's how I met her."

"I'm all right," Doyle said to Smith. "We'll hear the end of it."

"Not all that much more to hear, is there?" Turvey's fleshy lips parted in a smile. "You'll have guessed that the child's mine. Sorry to disappoint you in its parentage, Doyle, but maybe a known evil is better than an unknown."

"Yes," Doyle said. "I guessed that."

"She's smart. You have to give her that. She lets the news leak that Jan Teale's in residence at Bargehouse Mill. She's kept away from the village—only shown a glimpse of herself two or three times, just enough to get me on the raw and make me wonder what the hell was coming next. It'd have been money, of course. . . ."

Doyle looked at his watch. "It's time Tennier was here," he said to Smith, as if they were alone in the room, as if he had a mental block which refused to recognise Turvey's malice. "I wonder if he's upstairs?"

"Tennier will keep," Turvey said. "I wonder how long it would have been before she gave me a ring? And how much she'd have wanted on account?"

Inspector Smith knocked out his pipe and put it carefully into his right-hand pocket.

"Mr. Turvey," he said, "there are a few questions I'd like you to answer."

Turvey's head twisted on its thick neck. "Are you talking to me?"

"Yes." Smith's voice was matter-of-fact, the western burr almost friendly. He took a small diary from his pocket and turned the leaves. "Your name is

Norris Edwin Turvey. You live at Bridge House, Salchurch. . . ."

"What the hell is this?" Turvey asked incredulously.

"You travel a good deal, Mr. Turvey. Were you in Salchurch on the evening of Tuesday, August the sixteenth?"

"What if I was? I don't have to account for my movements to you. Or to anybody else."

"What make of car do you drive, Mr. Turvey?"

"That's my business."

"I'm trying to spare you unnecessary embarrassment. But if you don't answer my questions they may be asked again—by Superintendent Dymond. Doyle, what make of car does Mr. Turvey drive?"

"What's all this about?" Doyle asked.

"I'll tell you later."

"A Jensen and a Mark 10 Jaguar."

"Did Mr. Turvey call to see you on the night of August the sixteenth?"

"He hasn't been in my house for at least six months."

"But he did drive along the lane that night from the village towards Bargehouse Mill. Isn't that so, Mr. Turvey? You turned round there and drove back very fast—much too fast. You remember?"

"Look," blustered Turvey, "if you think I can remember where and at what speed I drove on a night nearly a month ago, you're even a bigger fool than you look. And if I could remember, I wouldn't be giving details to any interfering bastard who asked me."

"There was a drizzle of rain, Mr. Turvey. Now, try to remember exactly what happened."

He smiled at Turvey. But a subtle change had come over Inspector Smith, and the smile was as frigid as his level gaze. "*Exactly* what happened, Mr. Turvey."

Turvey licked his thick lips. "Say I was in Birmingham that night."

"Very well. It can be checked."

"Checked?" Turvey turned on Doyle. "Who the hell is this fellow?"

"I should have introduced you. An old friend of mine from Shilstone. Smith . . . Inspector Smith."

Turvey exhaled a long, spirit-laden breath. "Is that so! Well, sod Inspector Smith."

His eyes were bloodshot, his head down like a charging bull's, but something had gone out of him, in spite of his bluster. "You won't side-track me. The hell with what happened three weeks ago. That makes no difference to Wantage. Or to the scrubber he keeps in the top room. You start asking her what she was doing on the so-and-so of such-and-such."

He moved to the door and pulled it open. "You make a few enquiries about her, brother."

Doyle Wantage straightened up, like a sick man slowly recovering the use of his limbs. "This is only the beginning," he said. "Not the end. Don't have any illusions about that. You timed this well, Turvey. But I'll find some way of dealing with you."

"It's the end as far as I'm concerned. You've worn those rosy spectacles too long. All I've done is break 'em for you. From now on you see black and white. And I mean black and white. . . . She's a scrubber. I don't care if honey doesn't melt in her mouth in the chaste precincts of Bargehouse Mill. Or how she cooks your breakfast eggs. My car has reclining seats. Those rosy spectacles . . ."

He grunted as the bowl-fire hit him in the midriff—grunted and coughed. There was a stench of scorched cloth. A man and a woman were passing down the corridor. They jumped apart as Turvey sprawled back through the doorway.

The Inspector watched as he picked himself up. Satisfied that no great harm had been done, he shut the door, picked up the bowl-fire, and replaced it on the shelf. Doyle Wantage leaned against the table, both hands over his face. Realising that they were alone, he looked stupidly at the Inspector, shaking his head.

"I wouldn't have thought I could do a thing like that," he said.

"Many people must have felt the same way under similar provocation. That's one of the reasons I was always against capital punishment. . . . Where are you going?"

"I'd better try to iron things out."

"I wouldn't. It would make a bad business worse. Let it find its own level."

"But it'll be all over Salchurch, Smith. The couple in the corridor—they're temporary catering staff. Do you think they'll keep quiet about a thing like this?"

"Do you think Turvey will? There's nothing you can do. Nothing but sit tight."

"I suppose you're right." Doyle slumped back on the chair. He was unconsciously clenching and unclenching his hands. Smith knew what was in his mind. . . . Not that sudden act of violence, not even the prospect of a Festival split by Turvey's malice, but Turvey's venomous denunciation of the girl at Bargehouse Mill. And that was something the Inspector preferred not to talk about, unless Doyle mentioned it first.

"What was that date, Smith?"

"The sixteenth of August, you mean?"

"Yes. Turvey didn't like it. What did happen that night?"

"I'm not sure. I was following a lead given to me by a rather irresponsible character. The lead may have been worthless or my interpretation of it wide of the mark. On the other hand, Turvey may have made a singularly stupid attempt to kill your housekeeper that night."

"So—so that's it!" Doyle's voice rose sharply. "And if he tries again—"

"He won't. The position is quite different now. Though I shall mention it to Superintendent Dymond. It's his pigeon—if there's a pigeon at all."

Doyle straightened his tie, pushed long fingers through his hair. "There's still a time-table," he said. "I'd better find Tennier."

"I'll go with you, if I won't be in the way."

The Inspector sat with Doyle on one of the platform-seats while Tennier, morose and sardonic, took the orchestra through the Brahms, then tackled the Mozart with Colin Radwell. It was half-past five when he dropped the stick and came over to Doyle, wiping the sweat from his face.

"Anybody using this place tomorrow?" he asked, and Doyle shook his head.

"It's Maxton's recital and the Quartet at Luke and James."

"Thank God for that! It's your party-piece I'm worried about. I'd like to go through the score with you again, then I'll get the boys together tomorrow morning. Couple of hours should make a difference."

"I didn't much care for the Mozart," Doyle said with an effort.

"I thought Radwell was your white-headed boy?"

"I'm not thinking about Radwell. You pulled that last movement back till all the sparkle went out of it."

Tennier's dapper little body quivered. "You couldn't care for it less than I did, but it was a case of flogging dead horses. God knows what'll happen to Mahler on Thursday."

He called loudly to Carstairs, the leader, who was crossing the platform. "What went wrong, Bert?"

"Don't ask me. I thought you were beating time with a yard of candy-floss. It'll be all right tonight."

"Have you consulted your oculist recently?" Tennier asked nastily. Then, to Doyle, "What are you going to do till curtain-up? Coming with me to the pub?"

"I'll get a snack here. Where's Radwell?"

"Gone below. Do you want him?"

"Not urgently. Tell him I'll expect him at my place later. You too, Carstairs. If anybody sees Maxton, give him a lift. I'll probably be going home before the crowd turns out. What about you, Smith?"

"I'll attach myself to somebody coming in that direction. Or I can walk."

"No need to do that. . . . Are you going now with the others to the pub? You may as well. Afraid I'm pretty bad company at the moment."

"Would you like me to stay with you?"

"No, I've plenty to keep me occupied. Go and have a meal. It's a long time till eleven o'clock."

He watched them go, leaving him alone on the platform. Clouds had covered the sun; a few service-lights had been turned on. He rubbed his forehead with his knuckles. Curious, the feeling one sometimes has of coming to an end; of there being nothing beyond. Curtains falling, night falling, consciousness falling into a bottomless abyss. He couldn't easily think of Turvey. Even the man's image eluded him. It would be easy to fool himself that Turvey was still in Zurich.

He went to the cafeteria. The woman who had been outside the door when Turvey made his undignified exit was stacking sandwiches and cakes on the counter. He asked for a cup of tea and a roll. At six-thirty he went back to his room, bolted the door, washed and changed. He noticed that the rim of the bowl-fire was dented. Suppose he had killed Turvey . . . ?

Someone should have killed him long ago. His wife, or somebody else's wife, or some wife's husband. The image of Turvey, shocked out of his mind for a while, was coming slowly back. He turned off the fire and went up the steps to the auditorium.

The lights were up now; the Hangar had lost its look

of austerity and glowed with colour. The platform was fringed with autumn flowers, the gilt orchestra chairs had a Viennese look. This was a moment which, in other years, had never failed to move him. This was his own creation, living and breathing before his eyes, but now it evoked no response in him.

He had two seats reserved on the front row of the tier, at the left-hand side. He could hear the crunch of car-wheels in the park—early as it was, people were already trickling to their places. Singly and in pairs and in groups, laughing and talking. He went to his seat, and presently Inspector Smith joined him.

"Have you seen anything more of Turvey?" Doyle asked.

"Nothing at all. Maxton called in for a drink half an hour ago and he's still in the bar. Will he be sitting with us?"

"No, he likes to be over the other side. Ruth will be with him—his sister. This is one of the few occasions when they're seen together."

It was a pleasant night, if you were in the mood to be pleased. . . . The magpie-pattern of dinner-jackets, smooth hair against furs, an occasional smile from some-one Doyle knew, a lifted hand. . . . Here was Twelve-trees, thin, ascetic, looking oddly like an old rook, and Aumbrey with a set smile on his smooth face. Ebor Maxton too, with his angular sister.

One by one, casually, as if they had no conceivable concern with the business in hand, the members of the orchestra drifted through the doors flanking the platform. Chairs scraped, stands were raised or lowered. Doyle closed his eyes, listening to that cacophonous bedlam of sound which is sweeter than all the heavenly choirs to a man who has music in his soul.

The temperature had risen; there was a subtle per-fume in the air. He leaned over the rail and looked down at the amphitheatre. Plenty of young people—

God be thanked for them, the future's hard and enthusi-
astic core.

A smattering of clapping as Bert Carstairs came up
the steps. He inclined his head, he adjusted the gilt
chair to his liking. A long hush. . . . Then more hands
uttering louder applause for Tennier's entry. Shufflings
and coughs, Tennier's stick raised, a sharp tap on the
desk, the audience rising raggedly for the Queen. . . .

And the Salchurch Festival of 1966 had begun.

He came out after the Ravel. The night air struck
him like a wet towel. He walked down the deserted
street towards the riverside path. All that day, he had
scarcely been alone for a moment, and he needed to
be.

Doyle Wantage liked order in his life. Not in small
and trivial things; he would forget to wear a tie or post
a letter, he would work all night and sleep next day.
But he had to be certain of his beliefs, his sympathies
and loyalties. Now, he was certain of nothing. It was
a phase that would pass. . . . But while it lasted, he
lacked the courage to take a good look at himself for
fear of what he might see.

Turvey's poison was working, fouling his mind and
paralysing his actions. Years ago when his blood was
hotter he might have stormed back to Bargehouse Mill
and told her. But what good would that do? It would
be playing Turvey's own game. If only he had the
strength of mind to ignore what had been said. . . .
To deny its reality by an act of faith. . . .

At the bridge, he climbed warily down to the path.
There was no moon; the silent stream was invisible between its deep banks. But the village's reflected light
was enough to show the way to one who knew it as
well as Doyle Wantage did. He had forgotten the car
in which he had brought the Inspector to the Hangar.
Keeping well clear of the bank, he walked as far as

the lane and then turned resolutely homeward.

The house was lit up. He had told Janice to keep the doors locked during the Festival when she was alone in the house. He fumbled for his keys. . . . Hearing him, she came into the hall. He shut the door and stood looking at her. She had on a dress he had never seen before. For a moment he saw her through Turvey's eyes. . . .

"Are the others here?" she asked.

"No, I came on first."

"Is anything wrong?"

"Nothing at all."

"I've been putting the finishing touches to everything. Come and see."

He followed her into the long dining-room. When he bought Bargehouse Mill, he had acquired most of the furniture that went with it. The table gleamed under soft lights; there were flowers from the garden, and she had found the precious bits of old silver that had scarcely seen daylight since his parents' death.

"I don't know which is head of the table in this room," she told him. "But I thought you would be here. . . ."

"And where will you be?"

She pretended not to hear. He followed her to the door. "You still have that curious complex about making all things smooth for me and then effacing yourself, Jan. I want you to sit with me tonight, so if there are any necessary alterations you'd better make them."

She turned and faced him. "I can't do that."

"Why not? I know your methodical ways by now. You'll have everything ready to be brought in. Times are changing. Even Belgravia hostesses excuse themselves and fetch the next course."

"That isn't the point. There will be people I don't know. They'll wonder—"

He took her hand. "Come into my room. I want to talk to you."

They went in and he shut the door. He pulled a chair from the wall, but she shook her head.

"Very well, if you'd rather stand. . . . Don't look so bewildered! I'm quite normal. As near normal as possible in the circumstances, anyway."

"I ought to look at the soup—"

"If the soup burns or boils I couldn't care a damn. You've been here three months, Jan. A lot can happen in that time. For one thing, I've got to know you. . . ."

"No!" she interrupted. "You know nothing about me. Nothing at all."

"All right, we'll let that go. It's something we can talk about some other time. Do you know what it would do to me if you left me now?"

"I've no intention of leaving you, now or any time at all."

"That makes it easier." He noticed that the curtains had not been drawn. He pulled them across the window. He turned round and looked at her again, and this time he saw her through his own eyes and Turvey might have been dead. "Jan, will you marry me?"

Now she did sit down. If she had been bewildered a moment ago, she was utterly astonished now. "You— you're not *serious?* You can't be!"

"I never say things like that unless I am."

"But *why?*"

"Two reasons! I think you love me. You do so much for me that has nothing to do with obligations or payment. And I love you. I'm right on that count if I'm not on the other."

She was very pale, her eyes wide and incredulous. "Am I right on the other?" he asked.

"If only you knew how much!"

"Then it's settled!"

"It isn't. No, it isn't settled at all. I told you just now— you know nothing about me. I walked into this house three months ago. I've told you nothing, explained nothing. It hasn't been necessary. But you can't *marry* a woman you know nothing about. You can't, Doyle! Oh, why did you have to say this tonight? How can I stay now?"

"That's the longest speech I've heard you make in twelve weeks! Now listen!" He bent over the chair. "I don't care where you came from or what reason you had for coming. I want you to marry me."

She looked up at him, shaking her head. "I can't."

"Why not?"

"I've been so incredibly foolish."

"I've done foolish things in my time."

"You're driving me into a corner. I'll have to explain. And I don't want to—not now. I've realised I would have to tell you, but I thought it wouldn't be for weeks, months. You'll believe all the wrong things, I'll tell you in the wrong way, I'll be full of excuses and self-pity because I'll be afraid—"

"Of what?"

"Do I have to tell you? Afraid of losing you."

"I haven't asked for explanations. I don't want them. Not now. Tell me tomorrow, next day, next week. I'm only interested in you and me and the sort of life we can have from now on."

"Face value!" she said, almost in a whisper. "The times I've heard you say that."

"It's something I believe in. Look at me! Look at me, Jan! I'm going to put it to you straight. Will you marry me, and the hell with everything else?"

He thought she would never speak. Her eyes were fixed on his, but he knew she was looking through him, beyond him, considering matters that were outside his own knowledge. But unconsciously he had used the very words that won her over. He saw the beginnings of a smile; her shoulders lifted slightly. Life had been easy these three months. There had been nothing to light that challenging gleam in her eyes; it took him by surprise.

"I'll marry you," she said, "and the hell with everything else!"

A car had turned in from the lane. Its lights patterned the drawn curtains. He lifted her out of the chair and held her for a moment before striding manfully into the hall.

The Inspector, Tennier, and Bert Carstairs, the leader. . . .

Within seconds, another car arrived. It brought Twelvetrees, the unspeakable Aumbrey, and Grace Iles. She shook hands with Tennier and turned to Doyle.

"Heneage went for a last illegal drink to the Boar. I expect he'll be along presently."

"Where's Colin Radwell?"

"Ebor went with him to the station." Grace smiled frostily. "The dear boy was married only a few days ago and wanted to get home."

"I like the idea of Ebor speeding the parting guest! Probably Radwell doesn't realise he's blind. I wonder how he'll get here?"

She shrugged indifferently. "The station taxi would bring him back to the village and he could use it to come the rest of the way. But you know what Ebor is. He's just as likely to walk."

"What about Ruth?"

"Isn't she here? I could have given her a lift. But there were so many people milling around—it was absolute chaos in the car-park. I waited ages for Heneage before somebody told me he'd gone to the Boar. Stupid of me—I should know better by now."

Under his suppressed excitement, Doyle was anxious that Jan's carefully-prepared meal should not come as an anti-climax. He caught the curate's eye and suggested that he should fix up the first-comers with something to drink.

"In my time I've been many things," Aumbrey said. "Once I fancied Law. Three years I wasted on computer-programming before giving myself to the cure of souls. But never before have I played the barman."

"It will give Ebor and his sister time to get here." Doyle noticed the Inspector standing alone, and crossed the room to him. "You arrived in distinguished company," he said.

"You mean Tennier? He'd seen me with you and probably thought I was a kindred spirit. . . . You're looking a good deal happier now, Doyle."

"I'm feeling a good deal happier. I've trampled the devil beneath my feet."

He swept his guests with a slightly sardonic glance. Aumbrey was doing quite well with the bottles; Twelvetrees watched his expertise morosely. And then the third contingent arrived.

This time Heneage Iles came in with Ruth Maxton. A composed but apparently hostile Ruth, while Heneage was visibly under the weather. He gave Grace a glassy smile.

"Sorry," he said. "You know how it is."

"Yes, I know how it is."

He leaned against the back of a chair, owlishly regarding the earlier arrivals. "Where's Norris?"

No one spoke, "Where's Norris?" Heneage asked again.

"I haven't seen him since this afternoon," Doyle said.

"You can't start a party without Norris."

"It isn't a party and there's nothing to start," Doyle pointed out.

"Was Norris in the Hangar tonight?"

"Is anyone interested?" Grace drawled.

"I saw him in the bar during the interval," Inspector Smith said, and Grace laughed.

"He probably stayed there. He may be there now for all we know."

Heneage ignored the pleasantry. "What about Laura?" he asked thickly.

"What about her?"

"Isn't she coming?" He squinted from one to the other. "Nobody seen her?" Again he singled out Grace. "Haven't you?"

"I haven't. Wherever Laura spent the evening, it wouldn't be within speaking distance of her husband." She looked across the room at Doyle. "Did you invite her?"

"I didn't invite Norris. I took it for granted that he'd be here. Laura's always welcome, with her husband or without him."

"Nobly spoken!" murmured Grace.

"Laura," Heneage said solemnly, "socially speaking, has ceased to exist. When one member of a marriage partnership is overwhelmingly stronger than the other, then the other ceases to exist. It's as simple as that. Isn't it, Grace? I ceased to exist when I married you. Everybody knows that. Don't they, darling?"

"My God, did you ever exist in your own right?" she asked, and he shrugged his shoulders.

"There you are!"

The uneasy silence lasted till Doyle remarked that, apart from Norris, the only absentee now was Ebor.

"What time was Radwell's train?" he asked.

"Eleven-five," Tennier said. "He told me this afternoon when I mentioned that you'd like him to be here."

"It seems odd that Ebor should go with him. . . . Do they know each other well?"

"Why this unusual fuss about Ebor?" Grace asked.

"He happens to be blind," Doyle reminded her.

"Blind or not, he's a law unto himself. You should know that. While I was waiting for my dipsomaniac husband to return from the Boar, he and Colin Radwell passed me. They were going towards a waiting taxi. Colin spoke to me, and Ebor said that he was going to the station to see him off. It's as simple as that. Ebor delights in using the word *see*—you should know that."

Doyle nodded. "We'll give him five more minutes."

But even as he turned to go into the kitchen, wondering what Jan was doing, the bell rang and the outer door opened.

"Sorry I'm late!" Ebor Maxton said with ferocious geniality.

"Don't tell me you've walked," Doyle said.

"Why shouldn't I walk?"

Inspector Smith could see obliquely into the hall. Ebor Maxton was taking off his coat. . . . And the Inspector frowned. He knew, by some awareness that he could not have explained, that something was wrong. From that moment he was not merely Doyle Wantage's guest; the policeman in him warned him to tread warily. And yet he couldn't put his finger on the wrongness. It was a vague, irritating itch, but it remained with him through the rest of the evening.

They were seated round the gleaming table when Doyle, having trodden the devil underfoot, now proceeded to administer the *coup de grace*.

"You are all my friends," he said with a touch of irony, "and you know how it is with me. I dislike formal occasions. This year I've been able to dispense with formalities. I have a housekeeper."

He turned toward the door, where she stood, looking hot and embarrassed. "And tonight she'll sit beside me, sharing in all she has done for us."

"Hear, *hear!*" said Ebor Maxton, loudly and with great emphasis, while the Inspector watched Grace Iles' expressionless face and wondered what was passing through her mind. Doyle opened his mouth to continue, but Tennier was beaming upon Janice and congratulating her with heavy-handed mock-gallantry.

Ebor was not to be outdone. "I propose," he said, "that her name shall be added to the illustrious list of the Festival's honorary members."

"Splendid!" said Tennier. "By the way, you went to

the station with Radwell. What did he say?"

"We were talking about Arsenal all the time," Ebor replied blandly. "And I only shared his taxi so that I would have a prior claim to it when we came back to Salchurch. Wasted strategy! I walked from the village. My salary, a mere honorarium, doesn't run to cab-fares."

They were near the end of the meal when he raised his voice again.

"The informality you mentioned, Doyle, is greatly to my liking. Jan on her errands to the kitchen, then taking her place beside you—it reminds me of my youth. My mother, may she rest among the saints, sharing tasks and honours alike—"

"With the slight difference, no doubt, that your mother was married to your father," put in Grace Iles, and even Tennier looked startled and uncomfortable. The only one of them all who seemed entirely at his ease was Doyle. He gave Grace an unfathomable glance.

"I appreciate that, Grace. It provides me with the opportunity I've been waiting for. I still have a few bottles left that were laid down by *my* parents—and may they too rest among the saints! This is a special occasion. Jan—a moment, please."

She came to his side, slowly and shyly. There was no sound but the gentle murmur of the wine as he poured.

"Ebor, Tennier, Smith, Grace—all of you who wish me well! An hour ago I asked Jan to marry me. . . . And I'm very happy to say that she's going to." He lifted the glass. "Jan, my dear!"

The Inspector smiled approvingly. This was so completely the Doyle Wantage he had known so long. But he was still watching Grace Iles, and during the pleasant clamour that followed, his eyes scarcely left her face.

An hour later, as he was going up to his room, he encountered Doyle in the hall.

"So that's what you meant!" he said. "When your

position is too weak to defend—attack!"

"It was the only strategy I could think of."

"An act of faith, a gesture of defiance?"

Doyle leaned against the stair-newel. "An act of indifference, I think. Indifference to everything that happened before June of this year. I walked home. I tried to decide whether Norris was telling the truth or lying. It came to me quite suddenly that I didn't care which."

"I would still say faith, rather than indifference. I envy you, Doyle. Works without faith are dead. . . . Though I couldn't go quite as far as that. I think I would have to know. Even if it made no difference to me when I did know."

Doyle sat down on the second stair, briefly remembering that narrower flight at the top of the house.

"There's surprisingly little originality in any of us," he said.

"Are we still talking about faith?"

"We're composites of all those people who have scorched us with their malice or lifted us up with their love. For three months, we have been creating each other."

"You and the girl? Yes, I realise that."

"There may have been another Janice Teale before then. But she didn't exist for me at that time and she doesn't now. The human personality is new every morning, and I'm prepared to accept it on that day's showing."

The Inspector looked thoughtfully at his pipe, decided that it was too late to fill up again, and firmly put it in his pocket.

"You have an odd personal philosophy," he said. "I almost wish I could share it. . . . But I'm not sure that it would fit a mere policeman."

They had all gone, except the Inspector, and he was in bed. The dining-room was still littered, the kitchen stacked with the evening's debris. The only light was in Doyle's shabby room. The door was closed, logs burned brightly, for the marsh was rimed with early frost. He lay back on the deep settee, her head against his shoulder.

"There's no going back," he told her. "The die is cast, the Rubicon crossed, the bull taken by its horns. Can you think of any more?"

"The course determined," she said in a sleepy voice.

"Yes. Calm sea and prosperous voyage."

"In spite of gossip and scandal?"

"Lord, yes!"

"It doesn't worry you?"

"Why should it? I have a bullet-proof conscience."

"How she trapped him into marriage! Installed herself in the house, took possession of it, schemed for security and prestige!"

"They'll say worse than that, far worse. But nothing can touch us. Now, we shall live for ever. It takes two to create life . . . And to creat immortality."

"But he travels faster—"

"Ah, but who wants thrones or gutters? I'd rather have written any fifty bars of Mozart than conquered ten empires. We've work to do. My stock of years is smaller than yours. Swift to its close. . . ."

Long afterwards, she remembered the chaos in kitchen and dining-room, and tried heroically to rouse herself.

"Leave it till tomorrow," he said. "It's too late to bother now."

"Heavens, yes—it's nearly three! I'd no idea."

"Do you want to go to bed?"

"Not much. I'd like to stay here till daylight."

"I don't see why not, for once in your life. If you get tired of thinking about Mozart and immortality, you can drift away and I'll waken you in time to cook the Inspector's breakfast."

Tired as she was, it seemed a long time before she

did go to sleep. He too slept for a while, his head back against the worn leather. When he wakened, the logs had burnt out and he felt stiff and cold. Gently he slipped out of the room, and brought her coat from the hall to spread over her.

He was often out and about as early as this. He took great delight in those brightening minutes before sunrise. Dawn came in a grey cloud from the sea, and spread across the marsh like a living thing. Sunday morning—no post, no papers till ten o'clock. No need to worry about the world any more than it worried about him. He appreciated Sunday mornings.

He opened windows to let out the stale air, then began to clear the dining-room. The Inspector would not be stirring yet, and Jan, breathing deeply and peacefully, could sleep on till he had restored the house to something like its customary order.

Everything would have to be re-arranged now. He thought suddenly of Nina, and went quietly upstairs. She was fast asleep, one bare arm outflung, and he drew the covers higher. He could think of Norris Turvey now without passion—Turvey, who had raged so furiously and to so little purpose. There are rocks against which no sea can prevail.

Glancing through the landing window, he saw Tuke's jeep coming up the lane with the morning's milk. Jeff Tuke was driving. He turned in at the gate as Doyle went downstairs. Whistling cheerfully, he brought four bottles and was putting them against the door when Doyle opened it.

"Morning, sir! On the move early this morning, Mr. Wantage."

"It's the only time of the day I can get an hour to myself."

"Did everything go off all right last night?"

"I think so. Always a bit patchy on the first night, you know."

"It wasn't half busy. Regular traffic-jam at the bottom of Church Street."

"Were you there? I suppose not, or you wouldn't have asked about it."

"Not much in my line. Went to a dance at Shilstone. Nothing like a bit of life after you've had a week in this dump. Bad job about Mr. Turvey, isn't it?"

"What?" Doyle was picking up two of the bottles. He looked sharply at the lad.

"Scurvy Turvey."

"What about him?"

" 'Course, you won't have heard. Just fished him out of the river. Along Willow Walk."

"You mean he's dead—drowned?"

"That's it." Jeff Tuke pushed his fingers into the empty bottlenecks and dropped the bottles into a plastic crate. "Duck found his car and Turvey wasn't in it—"

"Duck?"

"Sergeant Donald. Got busy on the blower. Turvey not at home. Next thing, Duck sees him jammed against the netting under the bridge. Just down the road. Soon after daylight."

He slung the crate into the jeep. "Always something happens before Christmas. Bad job, isn't it?"

Doyle went slowly indoors. He put the milk in the fridge. There was coffee in a jug. He heated it up, poured it black into a cup. He lit a cigarette and sat down, staring at the wall.

Presently he poured another cup and laced it with cream. He carried it into his own worn room. Instead of drawing back the curtains, he turned on the lamp above his desk. He knelt beside her, watching the slow rise and fall of her breasts. Then he touched her shoulder.

"Jan!" he said. "Jan darling. . . ."

7

Found Drowned

Two constables and a sergeant were deemed sufficient by authority for Salchurch's needs. Young Jeff Tuke's report on their activities had been accurate so far as it went. Salchurch was normally unpoliced by night, but during Festival Week (when odd if not undesirable characters were in temporary residence, bars illegally open till the small hours, and traffic enough to waken the dead shattering the rural peace), Constable Palfrey occasionally walked round the town to assure himself that all was well.

It was during one of these prowls that he found Norris Turvey's car, unoccupied and unlighted, in Dove Lane, not far from the Hangar.

After some hesitation, he telephoned Bridge House. After all, four thousand pounds' worth of Jensen engineering should not be left like a student's banger at the kerbside.

Laura Turvey answered the phone and said that she had not seen her husband since six-thirty last night and had no idea where he might be. And, thought Palfrey, she seemed neither anxious nor particularly interested.

He returned to the car and peered through the windows. Nothing suspicious. Well aware of Turvey's reputation, he mentally reviewed the Dove Lane residents. Not one female under forty that he could think of. Nothing in fact within a hundred yards around that would appeal to Turvey's roving eye.

He went back to the police station and rang Sergeant Donald, knowing that he was on duty early and would be up by now.

Sergeant Donald was an Adonis among policemen; a tall, fresh-complexioned man with fair hair and a small fair moustache. He was not a native of Salchurch. As a staunch Methodist, he deplored Turvey's character, and privately thought that his permanent disappearance would be a blessing. But as a policeman he agreed with Palfrey that Turvey's bed empty and Turvey's car abandoned could add up to something queer.

He lived on the Marsh road, in the general direction of Bargehouse Mill. He was a man who firmly believed in keeping his eyes open. As he said, you never know, and promotion comes oftener by fortunate accident than by hard work. The truth of that was shown within minutes. Taking the short cut along Willow Walk, he observed the body of Norris Turvey jammed against the mesh of fine netting suspended beneath the arch of the bridge to keep the Salchurch Angling Association's fish from being washed out to sea.

Donald satisfied himself that Turvey was beyond recall. Then he walked more quickly to the police station and set official machinery in motion. Palfrey was told off to contact Constable Makepeace and recover the body. Then he went to Bridge House and broke the news to Laura Turvey.

She had just started breakfast, a frugal affair of coffee and toast. She looked haggard and bewildered, but seemed quite composed when he told her what had happened.

Donald assured her that unpleasant details would be taken care of, and she must not distress herself. What could she tell him about the previous day's events?

She could tell him nothing at all.

"Did he seem in normal health and spirits?" asked the Sergeant, remembering the phrase from various inquests he had attended.

"I think so, yes. . . . He came back from Zurich on an early flight, then had lunch and went out."

"To the Hangar?"

"He may have done. He was a member of the Finance Committee."

"And that was the last you saw of him, Mrs. Turvey?"

"Oh no! He came in about six, had a bath and changed, then went out again." Her voice was colourless. "I suppose he would go to the Hangar then, wherever he went earlier."

"I should have thought you'd have gone with him, Mrs. Turvey. I mean, opening night—sort of social occasion."

She shook her head. "I seldom went anywhere at all with him. . . ."

Her voice trailed away as if the whole thing was too obvious to need explanation. Sergeant Donald, an uncomplicated and kindly man, nodded sympathetically.

"Would his seat be booked at the Hangar?"

"I believe seats are always reserved for officials and committee members."

"Well then"—cheerfully—"the next thing is to establish that he occupied the seat and stayed till the end of the performance. That narrows the field, doesn't it?"

Laura Turvey agreed that it did. "I suppose he fell in?" she said.

He nodded. "It's a dangerous place. . . . I'll be calling again, Mrs. Turvey. About the—formalities. If there's anything I can do to help I'll be only too glad."

"I don't think there is." She gave him a ghostly smile. "No, not really."

He went away, sadly shaking his head. Speak no ill

of the dead. . . . But he remembered Laura Turvey before she had the corners of her mouth turned down as if you'd stuck a butcher's skewer through it.

The next few minutes were uncomfortable ones for Sergeant Donald. He rang Superintendent Dymond and told him what had happened. Dymond had an urban manor and for years had ridden Salchurch on a loose rein. He saw no reason to tighten it now.

"Shall I read you the procedure on suicide cases?" he asked. "Look, Donald, I'm a sick man. Overworked. I've every confidence in you. Try to be worthy of it."

Donald gently damned and blasted the Superintendent as he put the phone down. If things went right, Dymond would appear just in time to share the credit. If they went wrong, he would demand to know why Donald had taken so much on himself.

He went home for a second breakfast. Coming back to the police station he called upon George Meaken, the plumber, who for many years had sung alto in the Salchurch Glee Club and posed as an authority. He found Meaken in his back garden, snoozing behind a Sunday paper.

"I was there," Meaken said. "It finished at three minutes past ten precisely. I happen to know that, because I was working out whether there'd be time for a lawful gargle."

"I like that *lawful!*" Donald said.

"As for Turvey, I can tell you something about him that might be useful. He made a bee-line for the bar as soon as the first half was over. And that's where he stayed. He didn't come back to his seat."

"Did you see anything of him later, outside the Hangar?"

"I did not, no."

Farther down the street, Donald encountered Jimmy

Perrin, a sharp-eyed pensioner who on Festival occasions helped in the car-park. Perrin had not yet heard of Turvey's death, so the matter had to be explained to him.

"I didn't see nothing of him in the car-park," he said. "But that isn't to say he wasn't in the car-park. It's a big place, and it was darkish. Mind, there was two other fellows on the job."

The pursuit of those other two fellows did not commend itself to the Sergeant. Not at the moment. He was merely trying to establish—a term on which he doted—whether Turvey had left his car in Dove Lane instead of in the car-park, or taken it there later for some reason.

When had Turvey left the Hangar? And had he left alone or accompanied? Donald would very much like to know that. A nice point had arisen in his intelligent and orderly mind.

Mr. Doyle Wantage's friends invariably went to Bargehouse Mill after the opening concert of the Festival. Willow Walk was a short cut in that direction. But what reasonable man is concerned with short cuts when he owns the largest of Jaguars and the most expensive of Jensens? Turvey was the type of man who scarcely goes to the corner shop or even crosses the street on foot.

But with a friend, he could have walked through the village, discussing Festival matters, and they could have turned along Willow Walk because of its quietness and seclusion. The Council had provided convenient seats among the trees, and it had been a warm evening, though the weather had changed with the tide and it was now quite cool.

He made a short detour along Dove Lane. The car was locked, and a glance through the window showed that the ignition-key had been taken out. He returned to the police station and brought back a key-ring which had been found in Turvey's pocket; a ring attached to a fob which cunningly revealed itself as a naked girl when the leather flap was pulled back.

There was nothing wrong with the car. It started at a touch, and all the lights were working. So Turvey's late-night stroll had been a matter of choice, not of compulsion.

He sedately drove the car to the yard behind the police station, then sat down to think.

Constable Makepeace was keeping his feet warm in front of the fire, which was of that fierce and unapproachable intensity found only in police premises and the porters' rooms of railway stations otherwise freezingly cold. He looked up and asked as a matter of public interest if the Sergeant's luck had been in.

"No," said Donald shortly.

"I've been talking to my sister. *She* saw him. She serves in the Hangar bar. She says Turvey was propping up the counter from half-time last night till four minutes to ten."

"There's accuracy for you!" commented the Sergeant. "Not five minutes to—four."

"The way she keeps her eye on the clock when it's going up for tennish, I'd say she's right within seconds."

Donald said, remembering Meaken, "Did he go back into the Hangar?"

Makepeace was silent for a moment, then said, as if the answer paid great tribute to his intelligence and zeal, "I asked her that. She says no, he didn't. She says he went through the outer door into the car-park without even bothering to say goodnight."

"That pins it down a bit," Donald said thoughtfully.

"Pins it down a lot. *And* I've got another little tit-bit for you. My sister and her husband saw Mr. Turvey before then. Earlyish on."

"What's earlyish on?"

"Half past three, four o'clock."

"I'm not interested in what he was doing at that time.

It was six hours later when the fun started."

"Ah, but wait, wait! D'you know where Turvey was? In the corridor underneath the Hangar platform. Outside Mr. Wantage's door."

The Sergeant patiently lit his pipe and put his feet on the next chair. "My sister and her husband was coming on duty, getting the bar ready and all that. They'd 'ung up their things in the staff-room and was going towards the bar when they heard what Bessie calls voices raised in anger inside Mr. Wantage's room. Next thing you know, there's a scuffle and the door bangs open and there's Mr. Turvey trying to unwrap himself from a bowl-fire and a length of flex which to all intents and purposes as you might say seems to have been thrown at him by some other occupant of the room. Mr. Turvey falls into the corridor as if helped by a boot from behind, Bessie says, and the last thing they see of him he's cursing and blaspheming and trying to dust hisself off."

"Some other occupant of the room!" repeated Donald, sifting wheat from chaff. "You mean Mr. Wantage?"

"There was two of 'em. Mr. Wantage and another gentleman. On the stocky side, grey-haired, Bessie says. Nobody she knew, and our Bessie's got a sharp eye. Come to think of it," he added with relish, "we've 'ung men on less."

Sergeant Donald frowned. "I hope not. A row at four o'clock doesn't necessarily mean murder before midnight."

"Agreed! But coupled with the other circumstances—"

"What other circumstances?"

Makepeace became confidential. "Following this act of violence, Mr. Turvey returns 'ome. Comes again to the Hangar in time for the doofah. But the gentleman's so upset, and you can't blame him, that he doesn't stay long in his seat. He goes to the bar and fortifies hisself.

Leaves at four minutes to ten, having had a skinful. *And Mr. Wantage, the gentleman responsible for the violence, leaves the Hangar at about the same time."*

"How do you know that?" Donald asked sharply.

"Who was on duty outside the Hangar? Me. Mr. Wantage came out and stood there looking round for a minute. I wouldn't know whether he saw me or not. Then he pushes his hands into his pocket and off he goes."

"In which direction?"

"Towards Church Street. Which means towards Willow Walk. And Mr. Turvey wasn't the only one who had a bit of business last night that didn't need a car. Mr. Wantage didn't bother with his either. It's still there in the reserved corner of the car-park. Makes you think, eh? Makes me think, anyway."

Sergeant Donald made no reply. In spite of evidence to the contrary, he still liked to think that crime was confined to the lower orders. It didn't seem right to think of people like Mr. Wantage and Mr. Turvey killing and being killed. Or even throwing bowl-fires around, come to that.

Constable Makepeace was lacing up his shoes. "Glad if I've been of any assistance, Percy."

"Thanks, Charlie."

"Think nothing of it, Percy. . . . May a mere constable ask what's next on the agenda?"

"An hour of Sabbath rest, Charlie, followed by my Sunday dinner. By that time Dr. Greenways should have glanced at the corpse if no more."

"And then a Sabbath afternoon stroll in the general direction of Bargehouse Mill, Percy?"

"I think so. It seems called for. But I'll tell you something, Charlie—I'd rather run ten miles on a hot day in full uniform."

By that time, Doyle Wantage had confirmed the news which had come with the milk. Inspector Smith had retired to a sheltered corner of the garden and was looking thoughtfully across the flat fields. And Janice was preparing lunch.

Doyle leaned against the table, looking down at Nina, who unconcernedly played on the floor. He had just been talking on the phone with Ebor Maxton.

"The police have been busy this morning," he said to Janice. "I suppose our turn comes next."

"Mr. Turvey didn't come here at all. Why should they worry you?"

"Norris's failure to turn up may seem a significant factor. God, what a mess! I wonder what I ought to do this afternoon? Ebor will go through with his recital, of course. . . . I ought to be there, but I most certainly don't want to be."

That was an understatement. He shrank from the inevitable comments, the questions, the sly glances, the nudges and whispers. He had been prepared for all that in a different context, but coupled with Norris Turvey it seemed even more unpleasant.

Last night's emotional storm had not yet blown itself quite out. Apart from everything else, he wished that Turvey had lived long enough to suffer for what he had done—or tried to do. The Festival Committee would certainly have been rocked, for Doyle would never have served on it again with Turvey at the same table.

But all this, even Turvey's death, was a violent anticlimax.

With lunch over, he got ready for Ebor's recital. He might, after all, attract more attention to himself by staying away than by going, and Ebor would be peeved if he failed to turn up. The Inspector decided to go with him, and they were on the point of leaving the house when Donald's car turned into the drive.

Donald was alone. With one constable off-duty and the other at the station, he had no choice in the matter.

He greeted Doyle with respectful warmth, hoped that he was not intruding, and regretted the sad necessity which had brought him.

"Very sad indeed," Doyle agreed.

They were standing outside the door during this opening exchange. "I don't know whether you've ever met Inspector Smith in the course of your duties?" he went on ironically.

Donald looked nonplussed for a moment, but recovered himself admirably and said no, that pleasure had never come his way. "From Shilstone, sir?" he asked deferentially.

"Shilstone, Penrhuan, and various other coastwise hamlets. I have a large manor."

"This is quite a surprise, sir!"

"I imagine it must be." Smith's eyes twinkled and his west-country burr was a little more pronounced than usual. "But there's no reason why you should feel embarrassed. Mr. Wantage is an old friend of mine and I'm merely basking in a reflection of his glory for a few days. Let's see, Dymond's your Superintendent, isn't he?"

There was a subtle change in Donald's expression that was not lost upon Smith. "He's never seemed particularly interested in Salchurch, sir."

"No? Well, when I'm only six months away from retirement I may lose a bit of my own zeal. You'd better forget our professional relationship and call me Mr. Smith."

"Yes, sir, I'll do that." He turned to Doyle Wantage. "I've had a preliminary opinion from Dr. Greenways, sir."

"And it confirms the rumours we hear?"

"I'm afraid it does. It seems that Mr. Turvey died late last night or early this morning, and subject to confirmation by the post-mortem, he was drowned."

Doyle seemed to consider the point for a moment,

then suggested that they should go indoors. He led them into his workroom, glancing with a slight frown at the settee where he had waited for that morning's dawn with Janice Teale's head on his shoulder. Surreptitiously he moved a doll from the table and slid it into a drawer.

"It *could* be straightforward enough," Donald said. "I very much hope so."

"The thing is"—he settled himself on the edge of a chair—"why did Mr. Turvey use the Willow Walk path at all?"

"Why does anybody do anything at all?" Inspector Smith countered mildly. "I couldn't give a reasonable motive for nine-tenths of my everyday actions. That's why we have policemen, Sergeant—to provide reasons for unreasonable circumstances."

Donald regarded him thoughtfully. "I'll remember that, sir. . . . What I'm getting at is that Mr. Turvey's car was parked in Dove Lane. If he had wished to go home or to visit Mr. Doyle or to go anywhere at all within the limits imposed by ten gallons of petrol, he would have used the car. That's how I see it."

"You've checked that the car was mobile?"

"Naturally, sir."

"After drinking too liberally, he may have wished to clear his head and decided to walk a little way before returning home."

Donald nodded. His eyes moved from the Inspector to Doyle Wantage. "Before returning home, sir, or coming here?"

"I'm not quite sure what you mean by that."

"I understand you had a little party here last night, Mr. Doyle. Prominent people connected with the Festival in one way or another. As Mr. Turvey was closely connected with the Festival, I thought he might have been on your list."

"There wasn't a list. He's certainly been here on similar occasions for several years, but he didn't show up

last night. I can't pretend that I was anything but relieved, because I detested the fellow, though I'm sorry
this has happened."

"Was Mrs. Turvey also invited."

Doyle showed a trace of irritation. "No one was *invited*. . . . She's never been here with her husband,
though she knows quite well that she's welcome at any
time. You shouldn't need me to inform you that Mrs.
Turvey usually chose to stay at home when her husband
went out."

Donald nodded agreement. He said to the Inspector,
as if feeling his way along a thorny path, "You mentioned Mr. Turvey having drunk too liberally, sir. Was
that surmise, or had you some reason for saying it?"

"Some reason, yes. . . . He was in the bar when I
went down during the interval. He was still there when
I left, and in the meantime he had ordered two double
whiskies."

"Did you speak to him, sir?"

Smith hesitated briefly. "No."

"But you knew him?"

"I met him for the first time yesterday afternoon."

Sergeant Donald played one of the cards which Constable Makepeace had put into his hand. "Were you
with Mr. Wantage when you met him?"

"I was."

"Was it on an occasion when Mr. Wantage had a
slight—disagreement with Mr. Turvey?"

Doyle had hooked on his glasses, but now took them
off again. He was blinking rapidly, a certain sign of
mental stress. "That question belongs to me, doesn't
it?"

"As you wish, sir."

"If I admit that I had a slight—disagreement with
Turvey, you'll say *Ah!* in a voice full of meaning, and
leave me wondering what the hell I'm letting myself
in for and how long it'll be before you're back with

the handcuffs. If I say no, you'll confront me with evidence to the contrary."

Sergeant Donald removed a raffle-ticket from the sweat-band of his uniform cap, carefully examined it, and slid it back. "It so happens, sir, that Constable Makepeace's sister was passing your room yesterday when you and Mr. Turvey were having this—"

"This altercation?" Doyle supplied.

"You could call it that, sir. An altercation involving some business with a bowl-fire." He looked earnestly at the Inspector. "I feel certain that you must have been the other person in the room—Mr. Smith."

"And how many cats does that let out of the bag?" demanded Doyle.

"That's just what I'm wondering, Mr. Wantage."

At that moment the door opened and Nina came into the room. She made for Doyle, who picked her up and took her back to the door, conscious of Donald's intense and curious gaze.

"Jan!" he called. She came from the kitchen, looking with startled eyes at the seated policeman. "Jan, take care of her for a little while. We won't be long."

He turned to Donald. "That wasn't rehearsed," he said grimly. "My housekeeper, Sergeant, and her—adopted child. To regularise an already happy and rewarding relationship, we're being married shortly."

Donald coughed, and murmured inaudibly.

"Like most of us, she has a past. And as with us, it concerns only herself."

"A very reasonable way of looking at things, sir."

"I think so. And it brings us very near the heart of the matter. Turvey knew or claimed to know something about my housekeeper's past. He chose yesterday afternoon to display the contents of his nasty little mind to me."

"So that was when—"

"Yes, that was when! He chose his moment with con-

siderable cunning. He knew that it was the one afternoon in any year when I'm capable of going haywire
without any outside assistance. The strategy succeeded
very well."

"But apparently he didn't succeed in coming between you and your housekeeper?"

"He didn't. As for the bowl-fire, it was regrettable.
But I merely did what you or any other normal man
would have done in the circumstances. . . . Except that
your aim would probably have been better."

He took a deep breath. "I've told you all this without
being asked, because it would have come out in the
wash anyway. But I don't want my future wife to be
dragged into it. She's had trouble enough already."

"She won't be, Mr. Wantage, unless it's pertinent to
Mr. Turvey's death."

"I don't think it is. She was here all evening, preparing for our guests. Apart from that, she wouldn't have
left the child alone in the house. Not in any circumstances. So shall we go on from there?"

Sergeant Donald made a few sparse notes and studied
them carefully. He cleared his throat. "Mr. Smith . . .
You left Turvey in the bar and returned to your seat?"

"I did. I was sitting next to Mr. Wantage."

"So you won't be aware that Turvey left the bar at
four minutes to ten, and apparently left the building
too?"

"I wasn't aware of that."

"But, as you were sitting next to Mr. Wantage, you
will be aware that he too left before the end of the
concert?"

"I remember that he did. I can't give you the exact
time."

"Perhaps Mr. Wantage himself can?"

"I'm afraid not, but it could be checked. I came out
immediately after the Ravel."

"A few minutes before ten?" Donald hazarded.

"About that, I would say."

"Had you any reason for leaving, Mr. Wantage?"

"As a matter of fact, I had. I was still upset by Turvey's outburst. I didn't feel equal to joining in the general hubbub there would be when the concert was over. I wanted to be alone and I wanted to get home ahead of the others."

"You walked home, sir?"

"I did. By way of Willow Walk, to spare you the trouble of asking or finding out elsewhere. How did you guess?"

"Your car is still in the Hangar car-park, Mr. Wantage."

"How accusingly you say that!"

"Not at all, Mr. Wantage. . . . Needless to say, you saw nothing of Mr. Turvey during your walk home?"

"Needless to say, I didn't." Doyle hooked on his glasses again. "Sorry to disappoint you."

Sergeant Donald ignored that. He was making further play with his notebook. "Nor of anyone else, sir?"

"I didn't see a soul who could give me an alibi."

"We haven't got as far as that yet, Mr. Wantage. No one's accusing you of anything."

"I realise that! It's merely unfortunate that I quarrelled with Turvey, left the Hangar at about the time he did, and chose to walk home along the riverside path where he was found dead this morning."

"Unfortunate, yes!" the Sergeant murmured with evident regret. Then, more briskly, "Now, sir, if you could give me a list of the people you entertained here last night. . . ."

"There was Inspector Smith. There was Tennier, whom you will know at least by repute. Carstairs was here too. Ebor Maxton was here, and his sister. Grace Iles and her husband came—not together. I think that's the lot. Oh, Twelvetrees and Aumbrey. They lent an odour of sanctity."

"They all came here after staying till the end of the concert?"

"I imagine so. Certainly Tennier and Carstairs would stick it out till the last bar, though certain orchestras have been known to claim that they could play better without a conductor. I can't answer for the others. They arrived at various times within—oh, twenty minutes or so would cover the whole bunch."

Inspector Smith leaned forward. "As a matter of professional interest, Sergeant, what are we looking for? Isn't it simpler to assume that Turvey fell in? Must he necessarily have been pushed?"

"It's a point," Donald admitted. "Superintendent Dymond raised it when I talked to him over the telephone. I would have few doubts about it myself if only I could think of a reason why Turvey should have been there at all when his car was available."

He rose awkwardly from the chair. "Many thanks for the list, Mr. Wantage. And for your—frankness."

"Not at all."

"Now I'll have to get in touch with all these people. And on a Sunday, with the Festival going on, that will be quite a job."

"May I make a suggestion?" the Inspector said.

"By all means, sir."

"Why not question them here? Tennier and Carstairs are quite out of your consideration, surely. I fancy that most of the others could be got here on some pretext. What do you say, Doyle?"

Doyle hunched his shoulders. "If it would make things easier for Donald, I don't mind."

"I'm not thinking of making things easier for Donald. The advantage is that with all the interested parties in one room, one can sometimes assess reactions. In my own small way, I've employed the technique several times. It doesn't always come off, but one is usually better informed at the end than at the beginning."

There was latent respect in Donald's nod of agreement. "I can see that, sir. Will you give me a ring, if and when you get them all together?"

"I'll do that," Doyle said.

Donald was half-way to the door when Inspector Smith spoke mildly from the depths of his leather chair.

"A small point before you leave, Sergeant. You won't be surprised to know that we have been in communication with Salchurch by telephone this morning. We were in touch with Twelvetrees and with Ebor Maxton. I am told that Turvey's car was found in Dove Lane, with no lights. Is Dove Lane one of those backwaters where one may so leave a car?"

"It's a backwater," Donald said. "But the car should have had parking-lights. It would be daylight when Mr. Turvey left it there. I suppose he intended to come back later and turn on the lights, but if he was drinking heavily no doubt it slipped his mind."

"There's another way of looking at it, Sergeant. You wonder why Turvey chose to walk by the riverside when he had a car parked nearby. But to my mind, there's something very much more puzzling than that."

"Could you explain, sir?"

"I don't think Turvey parked his car there before the concert. You may be able to establish that. We're agreed that he would not walk a single yard if it could be avoided. Why should he park in a street some distance from the Hangar when he could have driven into the car-park provided, within yards of the main doors? Your problem is this, Sergeant, *Why did he leave the Hangar and drive his car to the place where you found it?*"

"I think you're wrong, sir."

Donald's cheeks held a touch of colour. It was the first time he had ever contradicted a superior. "I've been making a few enquiries this morning, and I'm pretty certain that Turvey *didn't* use the Hangar car-park last night, in spite of what you say. I'm just as

mystified as you are about his reason for parking in
Dove Lane, but there it is. I've talked to one witness
who says he saw a big car parked down there about
eight o'clock. That isn't conclusive, I know, but there
may be others when we get down to it."

Smith accepted it with good grace. So much so that
Donald coloured even more deeply.

"The problem's there, sir, which ever way you look
at it."

"That's very true. And it's your problem. I ought to
feel relieved about that."

"But you don't, sir. Do you now?"

"What do you mean by that?"

"I know the feeling, Mr. Smith. If there's any way
you can help—"

"What, with Dymond in the background?"

"In the background, sir. That's just it."

"I would certainly like to look at this riverside path.
. . . Preferably with a good local guide."

"I'll be free for an hour after tea, sir."

"Good!" Smith took out that thin-bladed knife and
began to clean his pipe. "Five o'clock, say?"

"About that."

"And remember," the Inspector said, "to call me Mr.
Smith."

8

Meeting Points

Inspector Smith rang Donald later in the afternoon, and arranged to meet him outside the police station. It was a situation with few precedents, he thought. Penrhuan inspector and Salchurch sergeant—it couldn't last. By tomorrow, Superintendent Dymond would have to bestir himself, and that would be the end of all such playful fraternising.

Donald was not wearing uniform. They walked down the street like old friends. When they came to the bridge, they leaned against the parapet, watching the dance of innumerable gnats and the swoop of an occasional late swallow.

"I can't claim to have an open mind," Smith said. "I'm quite convinced that whatever happened last night, Wantage had nothing to do with Turvey's death. That's where I begin."

"I wish I could begin there," Donald said.

"You can begin by keeping an open mind." He dropped a stone into the water. "Deeper than I thought. Quite a current too, though it's one of those menacing streams that run silently between deep banks."

Donald nodded, watching a drifting twig. "I don't think you need fear for Wantage. Guilt or innocence aside, it's difficult to prove that one man pushed another into the water." He looked sideways at Smith. "The best murders are done that way. The gentle shove off the crowded platform, over the cliff-edge. . . . It's when you start with three-minute alibis and rare poisons known only to the natives of Peacehaven that you come unstuck. . . . Shall we do down?"

They walked along the path. The Inspector's keen eyes roved among the undergrowth and the tufts of rank grass. "I don't think there's much in the way of clues," Donald said. "We've been over the ground pretty thoroughly. And this is a public path, of course—well used every day. There didn't seem any reason to cordon it off."

Two hundred yards downstream they came to the lower bridge. "That's where he was. Jammed against the wire."

"But not necessarily where he went in."

"Oh no. That could have been anywhere between here and the village. There's a smooth gravelly bottom. He'd roll along easily enough."

As they walked back towards the street, Donald said almost plaintively, "Am I being blinded by Wantage's obvious motive? Who else has one?"

"I wouldn't care to say."

"What about the housekeeper? From servant to wife in three months. . . ."

"She was in the house when Wantage arrived."

"Who can testify to that but Wantage himself? If he's infatuated enough to marry her after what Turvey said, I wouldn't put it past him to give her an alibi. Would you, Mr. Smith?"

The thought had occurred to Smith, but he had been unwilling to consider it.

"I suppose it's possible. . . . But it would have meant a precise timing and a knowledge of Turvey's movements that I find difficult to accept. It argues a previous arrangement. She would scarcely be foolish enough to lock up the house and leave the child within half an hour of the time when Doyle's guests were expected."

"He could have telephoned her or used some trick to get her out of the house. I'm not saying it did happen that way, but it could have done."

Inspector Smith shook his head. "I can't believe that Janice Teale could have behaved as she did last night after disposing of Turvey. She appears to me as being the motive rather than having one."

They climbed the steps and he took a last look over the bridge parapet. . . . "Shall we go on to Ebor Maxton's place? There's a sonata recital in Luke and James tonight. He may be staying after playing for Evensong, and I'd like a few words with him."

They approached Parvings by the private road which gave access to the school. Ruth Maxton was in her wariest mood, but Ebor greeted them warmly enough.

"So the police are closing their ranks, eh? In charge of the case, Smith?"

"I'm a privileged onlooker. Sorry we didn't turn up this afternoon. But Sergeant Donald arrived just as we were coming out."

"I didn't expect you. Not after what happened this morning. Or last night."

He stood with his back to the fire, motionless except for a betraying *tic* in his left cheek. "Has anyone seen Laura?" he went on. "I didn't care to go round."

"Laura?" Smith remembered the slender, hollow-eyed woman who had watched Ebor Maxton so intently in the church.

"Turvey's wife. Or his widow as she now is."

"I haven't heard her mentioned today."

Donald looked into Ebor's plastic eyes. "I saw her this morning, Mr. Maxton. She seemed as well as one could expect."

"Shock or relief—which?"

"I wouldn't care to say."

"I knew her years ago, before Turvey obliterated

most of what she was with the obscene stamp of his own personality."

"You didn't much care for Turvey, Mr. Maxton?"

"Who in this part of the world did? What's your role in all this, Smith? It was an accident, surely?"

"I think it was, yes."

"When's the inquest?"

"I'm not certain yet," Donald said. "Probably Tuesday or Wednesday."

"Good publicity for the Festival! What's the idea of the get-together tonight? Doyle rang me up a few minutes ago. Grace and Heneage Iles are coming and he'd like us to be there. We'll oblige, of course, but why?"

"There's always the possibility, Mr. Maxton, that it wasn't an accident." Donald was smooth and pleasant. "Suppose it wasn't, sir? Have you any idea who might have assisted him into the river?"

"Some hundreds of people, probably."

"What about his wife?"

Again that *tic*. . . . "If Laura had been capable of killing her husband, she would have done it years ago. Most women would—with every justification."

Ruth spoke for the first time. "My brother is quite obviously prejudiced in favour of Mrs. Turvey, but I agree with him there."

"And yet," Donald said with a wag of his handsome head, "you'd be surprised at the number of people who allow themselves to be pushed around till one day they touch bottom and reach for the bread-knife."

"I wouldn't be surprised at all, Sergeant, and I know the case you're thinking of. But thinking along those lines where Laura is concerned is simply a waste of time. I can't imagine why in any circumstances Norris Turvey should have walked along the river bank last night. But I can assure you that he would never have done so in the company of his wife."

"You have a point there, Miss Maxton. There's something to be said for the way one woman thinks she knows another."

Ruth smiled acidly. "In your position, I'd be more interested in Heneage Iles. Considering the position between Turvey and Heneage's wife . . ."

"That hasn't been overlooked, Miss Maxton. Anyway, we shall be able to talk things over tonight."

"A pity Turvey didn't die in Luke and James," Ebor said with his sightless stare. "You heard about that, Smith?"

"I heard about it." The Inspector remembered Aumbrey's story. "Though in the telling it possibly doubled its importance."

"Oh, I don't know! He could have died. . . . Panic, claustrophobia. Quite a fuss at the time. Wasn't there, Donald?"

"It was a bit out of my depth, sir. It wasn't till I took a look at the Luke and James organ that I realised how frightening an experience it must have been for Turvey."

"I've never left the blower running since that night," Ebor said with a chuckle. He added in his blandest tone, "It taught me a lesson."

As they crossed the playing-fields, the Inspector mentioned that Doyle Wantage had asked him to drive his car back to Bargehouse Mill.

"You've no objection, I take it?"

"None in the world. He admitted that he walked home—that's the only fact I'm interested in."

They parted near the Hangar, and Smith started up the car with some difficulty. It was an old model and the battery was flat. He steered warily into the street. It was a golden evening. People were making their way towards Luke and James; as a prelude to the sonata recital, Evensong was fully choral tonight.

A constable was on duty at the crossroads below the market square. Wondering if he was the Makepiece whose sister had so sharp an eye, he asked where he might find Turvey's house. The constable gave him a hard stare.

"It's Bridge House, sir. First turning past the church and it's the only house on the right. You'll have heard about the—trouble, sir?"

"Oh yes!" Smith said equably. "I've heard about it."

It was a Victorian demi-mansion which had mellowed better than most. Magnificent trees shaded well-kept lawns; there was a noble herbaceous border and a flagged rose-garden still heavy with perfume. He rang the porch bell, thinking that Turvey's widow might well be out or surrounded by friends. But she came to the door and opened it—a calm, self-possessed woman with features carefully composed.

"You remember me?" he asked.

"Of course! Yes—we met in the church."

"I'm staying with Doyle Wantage at Bargehouse Mill. He's an old friend of mine, and naturally I'm very concerned about your husband's death."

Her face remained impassive. "Will you come in? We have two servants, but I sent them home for the evening. I'd rather be alone."

She took him into the room where Ebor Maxton had sat with her so many times. But Maxton had only felt its warmth and friendliness. Smith had eyes to see the books, the flowers, the leaping brightness of the fire.

"You're my first visitor," she said, "since the police called for the third time this afternoon."

"I thought families closed their ranks," he said, "when a thing like this happens."

"I never belonged to a family."

"But your husband was a Salchurch man. . . ."

"And *his* family have lived here for generations, yes. But we've very little in common."

The green light from the window made her look old and haggard. . . . He remembered the younger girl at Bargehouse Mill. Give Janice Teale ten years of wariness, ten years during which she could never be her own generous self without a sneer or a blow, and she might grow very like Norris Turvey's widow.

"I'm connected with the police myself," he told her, "though I have no official standing here. I would prefer to leave matters entirely in Donald's and Dymond's hands. But I am by no means sure of their attitude, and one's lifetime habits of enquiring and drawing conclusions are not easy to put aside."

"You mean that Doyle Wantage is an obvious scapegoat?"

"At the moment, he seems to be. But there are others. Ebor Maxton's feud with you husband, for example. . . ."

"It wasn't a feud," she said. "They rarely met. It was the instinctive dislike of two quite dissimilar men."

"I was thinking of the curious incident that took place in the church some weeks ago."

"An incident, yes. . . ." Her face was expressionless. "Nothing came of it. Even if it had, what could it have been but an accident."

"Ebor Maxton," he reminded her, "forgot to turn off the electric blower. Ebor Maxton's hearing is exceptionally acute, yet he failed to notice a cipher—"

"Very well! Say that it was Ebor's idea of a glorious practical joke."

"And last night's tragedy?" he said. "Another accident, another glorious practical joke?"

"It was an accident, surely? The police think so."

"The police may have given you the impression that they think so. That isn't quite the same thing."

"It must have been an accident! It *must* have been!"

"Mrs. Turvey, there was trouble between Doyle Wantage and your husband yesterday afternoon over the girl at Bargehouse Mill. Have you been told about that?"

She shook her head. "I know about the girl, but I'd no idea . . . What kind of trouble?"

"It came to blows. This girl's name is Janice Teale. Your husband claimed that he knew her at one time."

A note of scorn came into her voice. "That must apply to quite a number of girls."

"You may be right, but I'm only concerned with Janice. She applied for the post advertised by Doyle, and came to live at Bargehouse Mill. A few weeks ago she was found in the lane between here and Bargehouse in circumstances that suggest that your husband had attacked her—"

"Or tried to rape her?" Laura Turvey asked without emotion.

"I didn't say that, Mrs. Turvey."

"He told me about it, you see. He said Doyle had a girl in the house, someone he knew quite well. He'd run into her, quite by accident. . . . it was a good example of Norris's technique. I would wonder about it for days. How strange that you should mention it!" She smiled for the first time since Inspector Smith came in—a curiously twisted smile. "He must have tried to rape her, and when he didn't succeed, he went to Grace. She would *always* accommodate him."

Smith was being taken a little way beyond his depth. "You mean Grace Iles? Did he tell you that he had gone there afterwards?"

"He did. Norris puzzled me that night. I thought I knew all his little ways, all the tortuous workings of his mind, but there was *something* that night—I don't know what it was. He was drunk, of course. He said I'd been wanting to divorce him for years—I could get on with it as soon as I liked. I asked him if Grace, then, was going to divorce Heneage Iles, and he laughed at that. He said I would find out in time."

"You took him at his word?"

"No. I suppose that seems strange to you. But he had a thousand ways of torturing me. I thought this was another trick. I've been waiting. . . . Last week I told him I was going to see a lawyer in Penrhuan—next Tuesday. I thought that might bring things to a head. He didn't even reply. I even wondered if he'd already started proceedings against me. That would have been like him."

"Had he any grounds?"

"No, but what he had could have been made to look like grounds. I wouldn't have been the only one to suffer."

"Are we talking about Ebor Maxton, Mrs. Turvey?"

"Yes, we're talking about Ebor."

He thought of Ebor as he had seen him only a short while ago. The touch of arrogance in him—the defensive arrogance of a man who is not and never will be as other men are.

"I could tell you," she said, "how innocently beautiful it all was. How I would go across to Luke and James when he was playing, and watch and listen and never let him know that I was there. How he would come here and sit in that chair, where you're sitting now, listening to the coffee bubbling and the fire snapping."

"And to the sound of your voice? You've a pleasant voice, Mrs. Turvey. The kind of voice I could live with in gratitude, I think, if I were blind."

Her eyes filled with tears, and suddenly she bent her head in a passion of weeping. He waited till the storm had passed, till her composure returned.

"Grace Iles, and your husband!" he said, as if that emotional outburst had never been. "From what I've seen of them both, I wouldn't have thought there was much common ground between them."

"There was sex," she said. "I didn't appeal to Norris in that way any more—thank God for that! And Heneage doesn't appeal to Grace any more. There's your common ground. Norris was born out of time. He should have been a sultan in the middle ages, and Grace would have been his head wife with a thousand concubines to keep her company. He's come home to me at night and told me in every lingering detail what he's been doing with Grace."

"You're free now," the Inspector reminded her. "And there are many years left."

"Yes. All of them lying under the shadow of this."

A month from now she would think differently. . . . But for her sake, as well as anybody's, the truth should be found, however deep the well in which it lurked.

"What kind of questions did the police ask?"

"They wanted to know what time Norris came home yesterday, what time he went out again, if I saw him any more after that, what I did with myself all evening. Things like that."

"What did you do with yourself all evening?"

"I went out about half-past nine."

Smith frowned. "Did they make anything of that? It's quite close to the critical time."

"They asked the obvious questions—had I seen anything of Norris. I said no, I'd already told them that the last time I saw him was when he left the house to go back to the Hangar for the concert. Oh, and they asked *why* I'd gone out. That seemed stupid. I said I'd a terrible headache and thought I would walk around for a while."

"But that wasn't the real reason?"

"No." She stirred uneasily. "It was masochism. . . . I felt there couldn't be anybody else as near to the Festival as I was and yet so completely cut off from it. I wanted to see the shops and the cafés lighted up, and the people and the cars. The ordinary, normal people. There was also the thought that I might see Ebor, but that was secondary. We were going into town on

Tuesday—that's when I'd planned to see the solicitors about my divorce—so it wasn't so long to wait."

"You didn't see him? Ebor, I mean?"

She shook her head. "I didn't see a soul I knew, except Grace and Heneage, and they didn't see me."

He caught at that, a straw in the wind. "What did the police say when you told them that?"

She looked at him blankly for a moment. "I—I don't think I did tell them. They didn't ask. They only wanted to know if I'd seen Norris."

"Where were Grace and Heneage Iles when you saw them?"

"You know the short new road they've made from the Hangar car-park to Church Street? That's where I saw Grace, walking towards the village."

"And Heneage, you said."

"He was a long way behind, hurrying as if he wanted to catch up with her."

"Did he?"

"Yes, and they started quarrelling about something. I didn't pay much attention—Grace and Heneage are always quarrelling."

"What happened then? Did they go back to the Hangar?"

"Heneage did. Or in that direction. . . . Grace crossed Church Street and I don't know where she went from there. There were so many people about." She paused, looking past the Inspector at the garden, as if re-creating the scene in her mind. "I began to wonder why, after all, I'd come out. It seemed so futile. I can't imagine what I would have done if Norris had seen me."

"Was this immediately after the concert?"

"Yes. People were beginning to leave the Hangar by all the exit doors. I came back home and went to bed about eleven."

Inspector Smith was prepared to believe that. But he wished that Laura Turvey, for her own sake, had told Donald about that late-evening stroll through the village. If the fact emerged later, it could put her in a bad light.

He said as much to her as he rose to go, but she shrugged indifferently.

"I don't think I'm under suspicion. I wouldn't have gone with Norris down the local lovers' walk. I think even the police realise that."

Inspector Smith had never been able to think coherently while driving. He left Doyle Wantage's car in a side-street and went down to the river-bank. The fact that Turvey had died there meant nothing; he sat there till the last streaks of day had left the sky and a thin, pale mist began to fill the hollows of the little valley.

Then he went into a small, comparatively unspoilt pub in the market square. It was quarter to ten when he drove back to Bargehouse Mill. By now, the gathering should be under way, if Doyle had been able to arrange it and Sergeant Donald able to attend.

Apparently Grace and her husband had arrived; their car had been left squarely in front of the door. Smith took Doyle Wantage's car into the garage and entered the house through the kitchen. Janice Teale was there, busy with a shopping list.

"Grace and Heneage, Ebor and Ruth," she told him. "It was a bit too intense for me so I left them."

"No sign of Twelvetrees or Aumbrey?"

"Doyle didn't ask them to come. Sergeant Donald phoned to say he'd be here about ten. . . . And he's bringing a Superintendent Dymond. Is that good or bad?"

"It could be either," Smith said, his mouth tightening.

He went into the big living-room. Ebor was standing as usual with his back to the fire. He turned his head as the door opened. "You, Smith? The local Super's on his way."

"So Janice told me a moment ago."

"Is anybody worrying?" Ebor asked.

Grace Iles, very smooth and composed, looked at him with ill-concealed dislike. "Why should anybody worry?"

"Why indeed? A clear conscience is better than chain-mail."

"The Superintendent isn't exactly a friend of mine," Heneage said, "but I know him quite well."

Ebor pretended to notice a speck of fluff on his brown jacket-sleeve, and brushed it away. "That may be useful. You know why he's coming? The police show neither fear nor favour, but they invariably arrange for the better type of cop to deal with the better type of suspect. When it comes to the Top People, they wear thin gloves."

He lifted his head as the gravel crunched. "Too late now for tears! Are all our stories well-rehearsed?"

Doyle brought the two men in. Donald seemed slightly diminished by his superior; his eyes sought out Inspector Smith and his shoulders imperceptibly lifted. While Dymond looked from one to the other, genially booming names as if each and every one of those present was his dearest and most valued friend.

He was tall and well-built, a man with a great presence. Grey, glossy hair, grey, well-trimmed moustache—he had the look of an elder statesman, and the illusion was heightened by his rich, plummy voice.

"Nice to see you, Smith!" he said, last of all. "Reversal of roles, for you of all people. Here for the Festival?"

"And as a friend of Wantage."

"A great pity the occasion has been marred in this fashion. A sign of the times!"

"What sign, what times?" Ebor asked. "People are dying all the time, aren't they?"

"They are indeed, my friend! All the time!" He sank into the largest available chair, murmured to Donald, and took from him a sheet of paper. He examined it in silence, till he was tolerably certain that every eye in the room was fixed upon him. Then he cleared his throat and passed a large, well-kept hand across his broad forehead.

"I don't think we shall find it necessary to detain you for more than a few minutes, ladies and gentlemen," he said. "Without dwelling unnecessarily upon unpleasant matters, I may tell you that the contents of Mr. Turvey's stomach point to the probability that he had consumed a quantity of alcohol more than sufficient to affect his judgment. One might incline to the view that he proceeded to Willow Walk in order to pull himself together before going home. With the—er—tragic result we all know."

"The unlamented dead!" Ebor Maxton said.

Those words momentarily checked Dymond's eloquence. "The inquest will be on Tuesday morning," Donald put in.

Ebor spoke again, ironically. "An unpleasant prelude to what should have been one of the great experiences of your life, Doyle."

Superintendent Dymond resumed his authority.

"Each of you will receive notification in due course from the Coroner's officer. Meanwhile, it would help if you would give me a brief account of your movements last night. You have already assisted us splendidly, Mr. Wantage. Have you anything to add to the statement you made to Sergeant Donald?"

"I don't think so."

"One thing does seem rather *odd*, Mr. Wantage . . . That you, one of the Festival's leading personalities—I think we would all subscribe to that—should leave before the end of the opening concert."

Doyle put on his glasses.

"It may seem odd to you. But as I told Donald, I wanted to be here when my guests arrived. Besides that, I wasn't too happy about the Brahms and I detest the critical or hypocritical comments that follow these first nights."

"And of course, one must remember the—disagreement you had with Mr. Turvey."

"Yes," said Doyle into the silence. "One must remember that."

"The disagreement—yes." Silence for a moment or two. "Then you walked home—by Willow Walk. You saw nothing of Turvey. . . . Yes, that's quite clear. And you, Miss Maxton?"

Ruth seemed surprised that her movements should be thought important. "It was the usual thing," she said. "I talked to a dozen people I knew and didn't know. I lost sight of my brother and couldn't find anyone else who was coming to Bargehouse. So I thought I'd go home. I was on my way there, in fact, when Heneage Iles came out of the Boar and saw me walking past. He very kindly offered me a lift, or I wouldn't have come here at all."

"And you saw nothing of Norris Turvey?"

"Nothing at all."

"Thank you very much. Now, Mr. Maxton!"

Ebor kept Dymond waiting while he lit a cigarette. "My movements were more complicated than my sister's," he said, "because I'm a more complicated character, but they're equally unrelated to Turvey alive and dead. During the interval I went under the stage and had a word with Colin Radwell, who'd just played the Mozart 24th and played it damned well. I told him I'd probably look him up after the second half, but there was such a hell of a scrum that I couldn't get through. So I sat down for a while till the tumult and the shouting had subsided if not died."

Sergeant Donald was making notes. He glanced up, expectantly.

"Long before then, I'd lost touch with my sister, so I thought I'd try for a taxi and come along here. That

too was a waste of time. With three local cabs and three
hundred customers I might have been there yet. But
Colin Radwell saw me and said he'd booked a taxi to
take him to the station. I could go along with him, keep
in the cab, and it would bring me to Bargehouse."

"A most cunning ruse!" commented Dymond.

"Cunning is the word. But as things turned out, it
was wasted strategy. When Radwell had gone, I remembered a score I wanted to show Tennier, so I asked
the driver to call at my home. Then the rot set in.
Couldn't find the score, asked the driver to wait a bit
longer, he came back with the number of customers
he had waiting, so I sent him off without a tip and
walked here."

"And you saw nothing—that is to say you didn't encounter—"

"I neither saw nor encountered Turvey."

Very guarded and cool, all of them. Inspector Smith
wouldn't have cared to say which was lying and which
telling the truth. Grace Iles, for instance—all the time
Ebor had been talking, she had been staring at him
with sheer incredulity in her eyes. But even that could
have been a pose for Dymond's benefit.

And there was something vaguely wrong with Ebor's
story, just as there had been something indefinably
wrong when he came in last night. Ebor Maxton did
not wait for cabs.

"Mrs. Iles!" Dymond said, as unctuously as if she had
been minor royalty.

"Am I next on the list? I wish I could be more original,
Superintendent. But when the concert ended, my husband said he was going for a drink. Like Ruth, I hung
around talking to people and feeling an utter fool, till
I realised that the Hangar bar closed at ten. Then someone told me he'd gone to the Boar. I followed him
there, but the car was locked, and I was in no mood
to go inside looking for him. So I returned to the car-

park hoping I would be lucky enough to find someone coming in this direction. I was—Mr. Twelvetrees came to my rescue. I'm afraid that's all I can tell you."

"All you can tell us—yes! Which leaves only your husband, Mrs. Iles. One excepts Tennier and Carstairs, and Twelvetrees and Aumbrey."

"Why?" asked Ebor Maxton suddenly. "Are parsons and musicians immune from the lusts of the flesh?"

"By no means!" Dymond rejoined smoothly. "But I fail to see either Twelvetrees or Aumbrey involved in anything as vulgar as murder, and after all that is what we have in mind. Perhaps Mr. Wantage could speak up for his musical colleagues."

He looked over Donald's shoulder at the notes. "If we could find even one person who actually saw Turvey going towards the bridge or down the steps, how much simpler everything would be!"

"You won't find that one person in me," Heneage Iles said. "My story is the shortest and the simplest of them all. I left my wife as she has just told you. I drove to the Boar and stayed there till Ruth Maxton saw me leaving and I gave her a lift to this house. Is that what you want to know, Superintendent?"

"Not quite what I wanted to know, sir, but if that is all you can tell me, who am I to complain?" He turned to Doyle. "You have a housekeeper, I believe?"

"She was here all evening."

"Ah yes, she was here all evening! Well, Donald?"

Inspector Smith contrived to be in the hall when they left. Dymond was talking to Doyle, smoothly, in the friendliest possible way. And Donald took advantage of that to murmur a timely warning to Smith.

"I hope Wantage has a good lawyer?"

"I imagine he has."

Donald glanced at Dymond's broad back. "So near to retirement! What a final burst of glory it would be!"

When the door closed on them, Doyle rubbed his

hands. "Now that's over," he said, "I think we'll have a drink."

Smith nodded. But instead of going back with Doyle to the others, he went into the kitchen.

That was where it had all started. If Janice Teale had never come, Norris Turvey would be alive now. A passive influence? He had thought so. *She was in the house when Wantage arrived,* he had told Donald.

And Donald's reply had been to the point. *Who can testify to that but Wantage himself.*

9

Triple Crown

With meticulous care, Janice was stitching a button on to a starched shirt. She looked up as Inspector Smith came in, and asked if the police had gone.

"Just now." He sat down, watching her break the cotton between white teeth.

"I could hear the Superintendent's voice. He *booms*."

"His whole manner booms." He looked at his pipe, then regretfully put it away. "Jan, I want to talk to you. Very seriously."

"All right. Talk to me!"

"The first day you came, you told Doyle that Nina was your sister's child. I imagined that to be a transparent subterfuge. I've always thought of her as yours. But now, I'm not so sure. I think you were telling the truth."

"I was. I wanted to tell Doyle more about it, to explain. . . . But it doesn't really matter now."

"I think it does matter. Not to Doyle, perhaps, but in other ways. Do you remember an incident that took place on the lane between here and Salchurch, a few weeks ago?"

"How did you know about that?" she asked, and he realised that he had shaken her.

"Through Aumbrey. I'm sorry to break faith with him, but this is developing into an ugly business and I've had to jettison my scruples. I don't think you came here in the first place because you like country life.

There was something else in your mind. Something connected with Norris Turvey. Am I right?"

She didn't answer. She folded the shirt and put it in a drawer.

"You don't often go to the village. But that night you broke your rule. Why?"

"Salchurch has a Festival Association. They were trying to increase their local membership. I thought I would like to join, so I went to a meeting in the Church Rooms."

"Was Turvey there?"

"No, but he had a committee meeting in the same building. I tried to slip away afterwards—"

"But he saw you and recognised you."

"Yes, he did."

"I won't ask you how well you knew him, Jan, or what the relationship between you had been. But tell me as much as you can."

"He said he'd known for some weeks that I was at Bargehouse Mill. He accused me of several things that were quite untrue. And he spoke very unkindly about his wife. Then he said he would run me home. Like a fool, I got into the car. Just past the bridge he stopped. What happened—wasn't very pleasant. I managed to get the door open as the car started again, and fell on to the grass verge. I suppose I must have passed out for a minute. Then Mr. Aumbrey came along. . . . Is that what you want to know?"

"It is certainly some of what I want to know. Meanwhile, according to Aumbrey, Turvey must have turned the car round at Bargehouse Mill and you had a narrow escape from being run down."

"It could have been that way. Even now, I try not to think of it. As for my relationship with Norris Turvey—there *are* reasons why I came to Bargehouse Mill, and reasons behind all that Norris tried to do that night. I'm going to tell Doyle, when I can find enough courage.

But it could be the end of everything. For one thing"—
she twined her fingers together—"I've been married."

That was more than the Inspector had anticipated.
"And your husband—" he said.

"He's dead." She said it flatly, unemotionally.

"I see! I felt that I was treading on dangerous ground,
but now it seems to be crumbling away under my feet.
Are you willing to talk about all this in front of the
others if I can find some way to break this thing open?"

Her eyes met his; they were frank, but lacking in
any warmth. "Yes, if you think it's necessary."

"I do think so. Shall we join them now?"

Ebor Maxton seemed more relaxed now that the police had gone. His sister was talking almost affably to
Grace Iles. Heneage, his Byronic head high like a well-
bred horse's, was saying that the police are usually quite
reasonable when handled the right way.

"They're doing a job," he said. "You can take it from
me that they pretty well know what they're after before
they start. It was quite obvious to me that Dymond's
mind was made up. He knew Turvey, he knows us.
He knows we're not the type to take the law into our
own hands."

"Well spoken, Heneage," said Grace over Ruth's
shoulder. "I'm glad you didn't mention your yearly sub-
scription to their insatiable charities."

"The thing is, they seemed satisfied," Heneage said.

Smith pulled out a chair for Janice, next to Doyle's.
"I wish I could feel the same," he said. "Earlier this
evening I was talking to Norris Turvey's widow. Nobody
in this kindly Christian community has troubled to call
and ask if she needs help."

He saw Ebor Maxton's mouth tighten. Grace seemed
subdued. "What prompted you to see Laura?" Heneage
asked.

"I like to hear various points of view," blandly. "Does
anyone here object to hers?"

"I don't know her well," Grace said distantly. "She's one of those dull, commonplace women you often find married to energetic, go-ahead men."

"I like that!" Ebor Maxton interrupted. "There are lots of commonplace women around. Conducting buses, nursing, selling bacon, stamping library tickets. . . . I like the type. I like it better than your type, Grace."

"I have no right to question Laura Turvey, or any one of you," Inspector Smith said. "But you can take it from me that the police are far from satisfied. Dymond soothed you. He was using a technique I know by heart. Next Tuesday, you face an inquest. You are in trouble, Doyle. Some of the others may be, but you certainly are. And I'm more concerned with you than I am with the others. You and Janice . . . Are you willing that the cats should be let out of the bag?"

"Have I any choice?" Doyle asked unhappily.

"On Tuesday morning, you may not have."

"Then let them out."

"And you, Janice?"

"Yes," she said. "However many there are."

Ebor Maxton grinned. "There you are! I like the type. The type that washes dishes and makes beds and cooks meals so that you intellectual bastards have more time to bitch up one another's lives."

Smith sat down, facing them.

"Being a policeman, I know more or less what Dymond and Donald are talking about at this moment. Their file is opened at Doyle Wantage. Recluse, living in isolation after a broken marriage. Along comes Janice Teale, with a child—her sister's child. She becomes not merely Doyle's housekeeper, but a charming, intelligent companion. Then, Norris Turvey steps in."

His eyes moved from Doyle to Grace Iles. "As a curtain-raiser to the Festival, Norris Turvey comes into Doyle's room at the Hangar and tells him that his housekeeper has merely made use of Bargehouse Mill to keep in touch with her former lover and the father of her child. He tells Doyle that it was part of a blackmail scheme—a plan to extort money or marriage from him, Turvey. He said so much that Doyle, mild a man as he is, lost his temper and threw him out of the room."

Smith's voice had lost is kindly burr. The eyes fixed intently upon Grace were stonily hard.

"The police know this. How then do their minds work? Janice Teale might be Norris's slut, but she was Doyle's angel. If Doyle destroyed Norris, then Norris's image of the girl would also be destroyed. Doyle knew that Norris was in the Hangar bar. Well before the end of the concert, Doyle left the auditorium and waited for Norris. By that time Norris was drunk. Doyle would say that he was in no condition to drive his car. Why not walk around for a while and discuss their grievances? Then—Willow Walk, the end of Norris, the end of Norris's Janice. *Now, there is only Doyle's Janice left.*"

Ebor Maxton blew his nose loudly. "Is there a counsel for the defence, Smith? I was wondering about the car." He blew again. "You said that Norris would be in no fit condition to drive it, and with that I agreed. You haven't told us why Norris left his car so far from the Hangar and walked the rest of the way."

"A mere detail. . . . What I have said just now, the police are already thinking. There will be a memo-pad on the Superintendent's desk—a short-list of suspects—with Doyle's name at the top. After all, who had the same kind of motive?"

He glanced briefly at Doyle, then his eyes moved back to Grace. "Who else had *any* kind of motive? Can you think of anybody, Mrs. Iles?"

"I can safely leave that kind of thinking to the police," she retorted coldly.

"But you must have ideas of your own. What about your husband? Would you think he had any kind of motive?"

"Heneage?" Her brows drew together. "Are you completely mad?"

"No more than I was a couple of minutes ago when I was telling you how easily Doyle could have killed Turvey. I had a lot to say about *his* motives. Shall I summarise your husband's? Or shall we revise your own account of what happened in the light of what I have just said?"

She made an impatient gesture. "I'm getting rather tired of this. I made a perfectly straightforward statement to the police—"

"And your husband did the same. They fitted admirably. Heneage said he was going for a drink. You waited, talking to people you knew. Then someone told you that Heneage had gone to the Boar. Who was that *someone*, Mrs. Iles?"

"Oh God, do you expect me to remember details like that?"

"Why not? It must have been someone who knew him, someone he'd told, someone who saw him there. . . . Someone! I am asking who that someone was."

"I don't remember." For the first time, Grace had momentarily lost her poise.

"A man or a woman, Mrs. Iles?"

"I resent these questions! If the police are not satisfied with what I told them, they can take it up with me or with my solicitors." Her oval face was contorted with anger.

"They will. In the Coroner's Court next Tuesday. There wasn't any *someone*, Mrs. Iles. Soon after the concert was over, you and your husband came down the access-road from the Hangar to the village street. You were indulging in a private quarrel. You parted on bad terms and Heneage went back towards the Hangar, probably for his car, because according to Ruth Maxton it was standing outside the Boar when she came past later."

The flesh seemed to have been pulled tight over Heneage Ile's face. "Where did you get this fantastic story?" he asked in a high monotone.

"Why fantastic? Yours was a good one, surely, till this shed a different light upon it. I suppose it scarcely seemed worth mentioning that you came out with your wife for some reason, split up for some reason after high words, and went back to the Hangar while she walked away towards the village."

"I never left the Hangar," Grace said distinctly.

"Very well! But don't be surprised if they put someone in the witness-box who's willing to swear that you did."

"It was much too dark for anybody to be certain," she parried.

"Exactly! Do you support the statement?" Smith turned to Heneage. "She never left the Hangar—is that true? Or is she for some reason covering up for you?"

"For me?" that roused Heneage. "What the hell do you mean?"

"It isn't far from the Hangar to Willow Walk."

"So you think that instead of going straight to the Boar I met Turvey—"

"Why not? I may seem to have a suspicious mind, but your flat denial of something that Laura Turvey saw and passed on to me in good faith excuses that."

"So it was Laura Turvey who saw us!"

He stared wildly at Inspector Smith, then made for the door. "The hell with you and your damned inquisition!" he shouted. "I'm going home. Are you coming, Grace?"

"Not yet," she said. "I'm much too curious."

She listened to the slam of the outer door.

"You've handled Heneage the wrong way," she told Smith languidly. "There's been an Iles at yonder house on the hill for more than four hundred years, and you know what close breeding can do to people. Heneage is an important person. You made no allowance for him. The Superintendent did. And you made one other mistake, Inspector. You shouldn't have mentioned Laura Turvey."

Inspector Smith opened his mouth to ask why not, then realised what she meant. And without waiting even to see what effect her words had had upon Ebor Maxton, he followed Heneage outside.

Heneage was starting his car. The Inspector opened the door, pulled out the ignition key, and put it in his pocket.

"Don't go to Laura Turvey," he advised. "What she saw, others may have seen. It isn't enough to silence her. Neither will it help if you follow Turvey into the river."

He led the way indoors, and took Heneage, a sorry figure now with bloodshot eyes and a hang-dog look, into Doyle Wantage's workroom. Before he had shut the door, whisky was guggling into a glass.

"Christ, that's good!" Heneage gasped.

"Dutch courage, but better than none. Now, what happened last night? Were you and Grace—"

"Yes, yes! I saw Laura Turvey, but I didn't think she'd seen us."

"That's a little better. What were you and Grace quarrelling about?"

Heneage shook his head. "Norris, I suppose. Norris was at the bottom of everything."

"According to Laura Turvey, you were following Grace, hurrying after her as though trying to prevent her from going somewhere or doing something. I'll make a long guess. Norris Turvey had already left the Hangar car-park and you thought your wife intended to follow him. You were afraid of what might happen."

"No," he said. "No, it wasn't that." But he said it without conviction.

"Where did Grace go when you left her?"

"I don't know."

He began to bluster again. He smacked down the glass on the table. "What can you know about all this? You're an outsider. What the hell does anybody know about what goes on inside the four walls of a marriage?"

"Are you talking about Doyle's marriage before you took Grace from him, or yours now?"

"Both!"

He was pulling off his tie, wrenching it out of the collar. All the things that had made him seem so young, so romantically handsome, had turned sour in him. The ripple had gone out of his jet-black hair; his sulky, chiselled mouth snarled, his Grecian nose assumed a predatory hook.

And quite suddenly and startlingly, he burst into a torrent of obscenity that matched anything in Inspector Smith's experience. Smith let him finish. The effort seemed to have exhausted him; he covered his face with his hands and began to moan softly.

"I'd like to rip her heart out!" he choked. "I'd watch them crucify the bag."

"You mean your wife?"

Heneage sprawled back in the leather chair. "Do you know what it's like to hate your own skin and your eyes and your hair?"

"It's getting late, Mr. Iles. But I've time to listen if you want to talk. She was Doyle's wife too, remember."

"What makes you think I want to talk?"

"I don't think. I know you do. Please yourself. You may never have another chance."

Heneage's eyes were fixed on the ceiling.

"Queer, when you think of it. I'm the seventeenth Iles to live at Salchurch."

"A good record!"

"When the old man died and I came back here ten years ago, I thought to myself, *Good, I'm the Iles now.*

Acres of Iles land around me, varlets and scullions who stared at me and waited to be ordered around. But I didn't know how to do it. I've never known what to do with life."

"You came back here. . . . From where?"

"I had a job in films. Scripts. I liked my job."

"A pity you didn't keep it."

"I know that. I'd four winters and five summers here. Alone in that bloody morgue of a house. Wantage was building up the Festival. Grace was there. I had to be pulled in. You see why?"

"You had the money."

"Yes, and Wantage had Grace."

"So you bought her!"

"It was more subtle than that. All Doyle wanted was peace and quietness. He got it. All Grace wanted was twenty thousand a year. She got that. All I wanted was Grace naked in the bed where I had been born. I got that. We obliged each other. Under the counter for a long time, then we made it legal in a civilised way."

"And how did it go wrong?"

"The same way it would go wrong for you if you had a wife who taunted you till you were mad and then deprived you till you were impotent."

"And then Turvey came into the picture!"

Heneage let out a long, shuddering sigh. "Turvey had advantages neither Doyle nor I enjoyed."

"Why didn't you let her go to him?"

"I wanted children. . . . There isn't another Iles coming up. And she had everything she needed. A triple crown. Power over Doyle—she never relinquished that, the Iles' kingdom, and Norris Turvey. A sex-symbol as blatant as the Cerne giant. But I couldn't let her go and I couldn't leave her."

"Can infatuation explain it?" Smith wondered aloud.

"No, it's more than that. It's like having a disease inside that can't be cut out else you'll die. I'm little, you see. I'm a façade. She knows that, and she doesn't mind, because I'm an Iles. I go with the trees and the park and the four cars. Anybody else *would* mind." There were tears in his eyes. "I wouldn't last a week without Grace."

Inspector Smith had an uneasy feeling in the pit of his stomach, as if he had turned a corner of wet sacking and seen something obscene and slimy crawling there. Now, he knew Heneage Iles.

"You'd better clean up," he said, "and we'll go back to her."

He followed Heneage into the living-room with the air of a prefect who has brought back a junior boy from some unlawful spree.

"I suppose everything is quite clear?" Grace Iles said. "You know exactly what happened last night, Inspector?"

"Not exactly, Mrs. Iles. But I've reached the point where I'm more interested in *why* than *how*. . . . And I think that is where Janice Teale may be able to help us."

He was beginning to feel tired. . . . Not only of that long hot day and all the things that had made it memorable, but of Grace and her husband and the posturings of all these people with whom he had so little sympathy. Doyle and the girl—almost all his interest was centered upon them, with just a little spilling over for Ebor Maxton in his dark world. He felt the need to shock them, startle them.

"Janice," he said, "what was—or is—your married name?"

"Myers," she whispered, "Janice Myers."

Grace's mouth opened suddenly. Ebor Maxton was straining his head forward as if by sheer force of will he would see and understand. But it was the look of utter astonishment on Doyle's face that Inspector Smith would remember longest.

"Janice Myers!" he repeated. "Teale was your name before you were married, I suppose?"

"Yes."

"Where do you come from, Mrs. Myers?"

"I was born in Bristol and worked there when I left school. Then my mother and sister went to live in London. I lived with them there for a while, but went back to Bristol as soon as I could."

"You mentioned your sister. . . . A twin sister?"

He waited. A lot might depend on her answer.

"Yes, we were identical twins."

"And her name?"

"Janette."

"How old were you when you were married?"

"Nineteen. I married an accountant—Keith Myers."

"You kept in touch with your family in London?"

"As well as I could."

"Will you tell me in your own words what happened?"

He tried to give the impression that he already knew the story. Actually, he was well aware that he had reached the limits of his own deductive powers and could ask no more leading questions without giving himself away.

"We didn't meet often. But my mother was constantly writing and saying that Janette worried her. She was—different from me, although we were twins. She came down to see me twice. The second time, she mentioned Norris Turvey. They'd been together in Villefranche. . . . Soon after that, my mother wrote again and told me about the baby."

"Nina?" Smith said gently.

"Yes. I thought Janette would take it in her stride. But there were complications and she was terribly ill."

She pushed back the hair from her face, a purer oval

than Grace's. "She was eight months in hospital."

"What action did Norris Turvey take?"

"None. She wrote to him several times. She never threatened or tried to make things unpleasant for him. She only asked for help—help that he could have given as easily as waving his hand. But he never replied. Then she had a letter from Norris's solicitors, telling her that these attempts to extort money from their client must stop, or further action would be taken. That letter came only a few days after Janette came out of hospital. Next morning, my mother took Nina in the park. When she came back, the room was full of gas and Janette was dead."

A tangible, brooding silence was broken at last by Ebor Maxton. "I hope he knew great fear before he died."

Inspector Smith looked at him, speculatively, then turned back to Janice.

"What happened to the child?"

"Keith and I adopted her. My mother wanted her, desperately, but she was simply not in a position to take care of her. My mother had always been very close to Janette—much more than to me. Her neighbours told me that she would sit there all day, quite alone, looking out of the window at the children on the street. . . ."

"Don't hurry!" Smith said.

"I'm sorry. . . . But I still can't think of those days without living through them again. We hadn't a lot of money. Keith had only a junior partnership, and we lived in a small house at Clifton and had a five-year-old car. But we both realised that we would have to do something about the situation. For a while, anyway, my mother would have to be with us. We arranged everything, and one day Keith drove to London for her."

She looked down at her hands. She moistened her

lips and spoke very slowly. "Coming back that night, on the Gloucester road, they skidded into a lorry. . . . No, Doyle, I'm quite all right. I've said it now, I've put it into words. I've never done that before. I'm all right now, really I am."

She was past all prompting now. The Inspector could only wait.

"So you see how it was! I was there with Nina. I'd lost my husband, my mother, and my sister—all because of one evil man living far away in a village I'd never even seen. There was just enough money to take care of us for a few months. In June, I brought Nina to Penrhuan. I had vague ideas about getting a temporary job. That's when I saw Doyle's advertisement in the paper."

"Why did you apply for it?" Smith asked. "What was in your mind?"

"I don't quite know. The advertisement said Salchurch, a mile out of the village. I thought that perhaps I could make Norris Turvey afraid. I didn't think he would know that Janette was dead. She wouldn't have told him much about me—she never talked about her family. She was always called Jan, and so was I. So if Jan Teale and her little girl came to Salchurch, if they never tried to get in touch with him, if they were simply *here*—you see?"

"A war of nerves!"

"Yes. Then everything began to change. The peace, the quietness. . . . And Doyle's kindness. I couldn't believe I had ever been so foolish. Norris didn't matter any more. What did matter was the difficulty of explaining it all to Doyle. I couldn't bring myself to do it. I knew he hated lies and deceit. I couldn't be sure what would happen when he knew."

"But you're sure now?"

Doyle Wantage spoke for her. "Yes, she's sure now.

Christ, she could have been sure then!"

"But the damage was done!" the Inspector said. "It was common knowledge in the village that a girl called Teale was at Bargehouse Mill with a three-year-old child. What happened that night in the lane, Janice?"

"He was puzzled. I was the girl he knew, and yet I was different. He said that when I wrote to him he was in an awkward position. He wished now that he had admitted the child was his and let his wife divorce him."

"Did he mention Grace Iles?"

"Yes. He must have talked to Janette about her."

"What did he say?"

"He said that—that he was tired of her."

Grace rose slowly to her feet. "You unspeakable little slut!"

"I asked for the information," Smith said tersely.

"And she wrapped it up nicely," Ebor Maxton snapped. "If I ever knew Norris, he'd say you're running to fat. For Norris, the accent was always on youth."

"If you can disregard these interruptions, Janice. . . ."

"He said that he could dispose of his holdings in the firm and we could go to Brazil or South Africa. By that time I was really scared. I'm certain he had no idea at all that Janette was dead. He made some rather clumsy attempts—but that doesn't matter either. I said yes, yes, I was willing to do anything he said. All I wanted was to get out of the car."

"And fortunately you did get out. And so, once again, Grace Iles becomes the dominant figure."

"I?" Grace stood up, a defiant, scornful figure. "What have I to do with this melodramatic, heart-tearing story?"

Smith turned very slowly to face her. All his antagonism seemed to be focused upon her.

"Norris Turvey went home that night and told his

wife that he wanted her to divorce him. He also told her why, and what he said corresponds strikingly with Janice's story. A girl he knew was in Doyle Wantage's house. Even then, Laura Turvey failed to realise that this girl was his reason for wanting a divorce. She asked if Grace was also getting a divorce—from Heneage—and the question seemed to amuse him. *He told Laura that he had been with Grace for the past two hours."*

He paused to marshal his facts. He should have taken notes, he thought. . . . He was reminded of those Penrhuan preachers who, in his youth, had declaimed for an hour on death, judgement, and the life to come with almost as little good solid material to build on.

"You appreciate the sequence? Turvey, drunk and lecherous, has the scene in his car with Janette—or the girl he believes to be Janette. He suggests that they leave the country. Next, still drunk, he spends two hours with Grace Iles. Then he goes home and invites his wife to divorce him. The second period is of more interest to me than the other two. What did he tell Grace herself? In those two hours he spent with her, you have the key to all that happened last night."

Heneage found his voice. "As your husband," he said, "I forbid you to say a word until you've taken legal advice."

"You *forbid* me? Heneage, for God's sake try to be your age!"

"I knew nothing about this. You didn't tell me that Norris was contemplating a divorce."

"When did I ever tell you anything at all about Norris?" she demanded icily.

Smith rapped his knuckles on the table. "Do you wish to talk about this, Mrs. Iles? Or do you prefer to take your legal-minded husband's advice?"

"I have nothing to say."

"Very well! I shall take all this to Dymond, tomorrow morning."

"And what is *your* motive, Inspector Smith? Consideration for me, or something more subtle?"

"I'm not a subtle man. I only want it to be known that neither Doyle Wantage nor Janice Teale had any hand in Turvey's death. That means knowing who had. Shall we go on from there?"

"I have nothing to say." Again she told him that, stubbornly.

"Let me help. On the night that Janice had her unpleasant experience with Turvey, you saw her leave with him?"

"Of course I did."

"You waited till he came back?"

"I wasn't even sure that he would come back. I did walk a little way towards Bargehouse Mill."

"And met him. Where did you spend the next two hours?"

"In his car. We drove towards the coast road."

"And he told you, roughly, what he told his wife later. He left you in no doubt that young Janette Teale was a more attractive proposition in every way than you were. He told you he was about to ask his wife for a divorce. You saw a third of your kingdom slipping. The third that supplied the butter for Heneage's dry bread, the sexual stimulus that made life with Heneage bearable. He probably reminded you of your age. . ."

"Damn you, Smith!" Heneage thrust in between them. "Grace, I don't care what he or anyone else says. I'm willing to forgive you. I don't care what you've done."

"That's wonderful, Heneage! I appreciate it so very much! Did Norris carry out his threat before he died?"

There was a split in Grace's smooth façade; she had reached the limit of some inward pressure. Heneage, completely bewildered, was shaking his head.

"Threat?" he repeated. "What threat?"

"Norris's last words to me that night were that his

parting gift to my husband would be the hotel bill he settled at Littlehampton in April."

Heneage pushed the hair out of his eyes. "But you were in Edinburgh. I drove you to Exeter and you caught a train there. *You were in Edinburgh. . . .*"

"For eleven days," she said, "I was with Norris in Littlehampton."

"But why bring that up?" Heneage said. "Why, at a time like this?"

"I'm intelligent enough to realise that I'm slowly being driven into a corner. Call it self-justification if you like."

Smith continued the offensive. "You said goodbye to Turvey on that pleasant note, Mrs. Iles. When did you see him again?"

"As he was leaving the Hangar, yesterday afternoon."

"A casual meeting?"

"Oh quite! I'd rung him three times a day at home, I'd tried to get in touch with him at the office. I'd even written to him."

"Why?" asked Ebor Maxton from his darkness: "Don't tell me *you* were expecting a child? He seemed to reserve that kind of treatment for members of his seraglio."

Her eyes glittered as she met Ebor's sightless stare. "No, I only wish I'd been that sort of woman."

10

With Murder in Mind

"Would you like a drink, Grace?" asked Doyle.

"I can manage without one, thanks. So long as your friend doesn't keep it up too long."

There had been a general stirring, a relief from tension. It was a mere hiatus. No one looked at the Inspector, not even Janice. Like the bearer of bad tidings, he was momentarily shunned.

Oddly, Grace needed no prompting now. In some way she was mistress of the situation; she had been made to talk, and she would talk as she pleased.

"When I met Norris outside the Hangar," she said, "I asked where he was going. He said back home, for a meal and a bath. He had only arrived back from Zurich a few hours before."

"Did he say any more about his divorce, or about his intention to go away with Janice?"

"No. I wanted to talk to him about that, but he said there were too many people around and he was in a hurry. I reminded him that we would be expected at Doyle's that night, after the concert, and I couldn't face the girl—I had to talk to him before then. He said very well—he wasn't bringing Laura here. I could lose Heneage after the concert, go to his car, and we would talk on our way here."

"What went wrong, Mrs. Iles?"

Her full red lips parted and twisted in a clown's

bloated smile. "Norris had no intention of meeting me or bringing me here. I knew he was in the bar. The moment the concert was over I slipped away from Heneage and went to the car-park. Norris always put his car in the same place. There's a space reserved for official use. But the car wasn't there."

"Because he had parked it in Dove Lave, well away from the Hangar!"

"Yes." .

"Why did he do that—to avoid meeting you?"

"I suppose so. I hurried back to the bar, but it was closed. I could only think that he might have gone home. I was very upset, and that was rather frightening, because I am not the type of person to get upset about things like that. Heneage saw me as I was hurrying away from the Hangar after making sure that Norris wasn't in the bar. He must have realised that something was wrong. I made some excuse, but he followed me down the access-road and there was quite a scene before I finally got away from him."

Smith glanced at Doyle. "Confirmation for Laura Turvey's story! Where did you go, Mrs. Iles, when you left your husband?"

"I thought he might have gone home, and I was in the mood to follow him there, whatever Laura might think. I went along Dove Lane and saw the car—and Norris himself. He was starting to unlock the door when he saw me."

Grace frowned. "I surprised myself. I made quite a scene. I behaved like any cheap tart who's been thrown over for another woman. Norris panicked—I must be rather alarming when I let myself go. He struck me across the mouth, and that quietened me. He said if we *had* to talk, we'd better find some quiet place and get things straightened out. He wanted me to get in the car, but I wouldn't do that. I had a violent headache and my mouth was bleeding. I wanted to stay out in the cool air. Besides, I had so many memories of that car, and I knew Norris too well. Once I got into the car, he was quite capable of driving straight here without any attempt to talk things over at all."

"So you went to Willow Walk?" Smith suggested.

"We did that. I don't remember much of what we talked about on the way. Not till we came to the bridge and went down the steps to the Walk."

She sat down again and took a cigarette from a small gold case. Heneage lit it for her. She didn't even glance at him.

"I remember telling Norris that the arrangement between us had suited me very well indeed, and I'd thought it would go on indefinitely. . . . I made the mistake of admitting to Norris that he was necessary to me."

"And he laughed at that?"

"He laughed like hell! I reminded him that he'd sometimes talked about letting Laura divorce him, and I'd thought it was so that *we* could be together. . . . No, Heneage, for God's sake don't come near me! I always loathed you in a loyal, sympathetic mood! I said to him, *why* this girl? I said why sacrifice everything for a little whore he'd slept with a few times years ago? I asked him for one reason—just one. And that's when he signed his own death-warrant. He said he would. . . . She didn't wear a girdle."

"And that," Smith said, "was when you pushed him into the river!"

She smiled and shook her head. "You'd like me to say that, wouldn't you? That I pushed him in and I'd do it again, a thousand times? But I'm a little too cautious for that, Inspector Smith. I'm only prepared to say that he put his hands on my shoulders and began to shake me, and I found the stench of second-hand whisky so offensive that I pushed him away, and he—slipped."

"And he couldn't swim! You probably discovered that at Littlehampton, Mrs. Iles? How fortunate for you that there were no witnesses!"

"There was one," she retorted cuttingly. "Going back to the road I passed Ebor Maxton—on his way here, I suppose." She threw her cigarette into the fire. "But naturally, he didn't see me. It took only a few minutes to reach the car-park. I saw Twelvetrees and told him I couldn't find Heneage or our car, and he very kindly brought me here."

She faced the Inspector squarely. "So what are you going to do?"

"I want to think about that," Smith told her.

"You realise that if this epic of lust and murder reached the ears of the police, I should deny it? My statement—my *official* statement—is already in their hands. If I were questioned, I should say that Norris never meant anything to me, except as a bottomless coffer for the Festival's demands. That I am not and never was the woman scorned, and that my waist-line scarcely interests me. I did not see Norris last night. When I hurried away from the Hangar, I was looking for Colin Radwell, because I would like him to stay with us next weekend when he comes down to play the Emperor. And the argument with my husband arose because I'd come out of the Hangar without even a wrap. Isn't that so, Heneage?"

"Certainly!" he agreed. "I was afraid you'd take a chill."

She smiled indulgently. "Dear Heneage! And now, I'd like to go home, please."

When they had gone, leaving Ebor and his sister to be driven home by Doyle, the Inspector took the drink Janice gave him. "I wonder!" he said. "All that, and the chances are that she'll go scot-free."

"Scot-free?" Ebor Maxton echoed. "In that little hell

the two of them share? Night and day, supper and breakfast with Turvey's drowned body between them?"

Unerringly he came to Janice and tilted up her face. "It's been a long day," he said. He stooped and kissed her forehead. "A long, long day!"

Envoi

On Tuesday afternoon, Inspector Smith accompanied Ebor Maxton back to the village after a session of sòmbre conversation at Bargehouse Mill. The inquest had come and gone, and little else had been talked about by the subdued group gathered around the fire in Doyle's room.

"Accidental Death!" the Inspector said as they turned along the winding riverside path. "I still find it difficult to believe."

They came to a gate, bleached grey by wind and rain. Ebor leaned against it, running his hands along the rough wooden rail.

"I often stand here," he said. "Strange, but the wind always seems to blow from the west. I like to feel it on my face."

"It's a soft wind today." Smith stood close beside him. "More like spring than autumn."

"Can we see the Hangar from here?"

"Beyond the trees, yes."

"You'll be there tonight?"

"I hope to be."

"*Tantae molis erat!* The night of his triumph. And nothing now will dim it! I find it easy to talk to you, Smith. It's unlikely that we shall often meet now all this is over and done with. We know the verdict. What do you think of Grace's remarkable performance on Sunday night?"

"It's something I shall never quite understand."

"I've thought about it a good deal. Her pride had taken a bitter blow. We knew what Norris had done to her. So she told us how she had made him pay. She justified herself, but in such a way that it can never be brought home to her. A push in disgust, in self-defence, or with murder in mind—who can say? But she did kill him, Smith, and she killed him deliberately."

"How can you be so sure?"

"Because Norris Turvey himself told me."

"Is this a macabre joke?"

"No. I'm not the man to wait for cars and taxis, Smith—you should know that. I set off to walk to Doyle's place immediately the concert was over. Within a few yards of this place, Grace passed me, hurrying towards the village. I could speak of the length of her stride, the weight of her footfalls, but let us say that I *knew*. And a few moments later I heard Turvey crying for help."

"So that was why she looked at you so often. . . . She was wondering—"

"I don't know. She may have been."

"You knew it was Turvey?"

"Not at that moment. Even I can't recognise the gurglings of a man half-submerged in cold water, a man clinging for life to a handful of twigs that overhung the stream. I pulled off my coat and went in."

"*You?* As you are?"

"I may not be able to see, but I can swim. Reasonably well, though the current and Turvey's weight proved too much for me. I used the last of my strength in keeping his head above water, and he used the last of his breath in telling me with obscene emphasis that Grace had pushed him in. I held him there for a full minute before I had to let him go, then I had the devil's own job to scramble up the bank myself."

"This seems to make the whole thing even more appalling than before."

"You think so? For once, I was at a loss. I found my coat, and fortunately there was a scarf in one of the pockets. Apart from leaving a damp trail wherever I went, I could conceal my plight. I went back towards the Hangar, hoping that my sister would see me. Ruth's a self-righteous bitch, but she has a sense of family. Unfortunately, it was Colin Radwell who spotted me. I made some excuse about looking for a taxi, and he invited me to share his. I explained that during the general confession. I wonder if the taxi-driver had complaints about water on the floor?"

He scrabbled for a stone and pitched it into the little river. "Deep and treacherous! Like Grace Iles. . . . My reason for calling at home after going with Radwell to the station should be obvious."

"To change your clothes, of course?"

"The quickest change I ever remember making."

"I knew something was wrong when you came into Bargehouse Mill on Saturday night. I'd been talking to you in the Hangar. There was some difference in your appearance that I couldn't help noticing, and yet its origin eluded me. I should have realised that you were wearing a different suit."

They walked back along the path and climbed the steps. "Why did you trouble to conceal all this?" Smith asked.

Ebor's head tilted in that familiar pose of attentiveness. "Is anyone within earshot?"

"We have the street to ourselves."

"Then I'll tell you . . . Or ask you. Smith, who killed him—Grace who pushed him in, or I who let him go?"

"There's a considerable difference, surely."

"You think so? But remember that I detested the man with my whole being. As I held him there, I was remembering what he'd done to his wife. Today, Laura and I should have gone to town. She hadn't told me her reasons for going—that she was starting divorce proceedings. She wouldn't want me to build up on it and then have my hopes shattered. But if she had told me, I think Turvey would be alive now."

"A sobering thought!" the Inspector said in a troubled voice.

"I held him there, Smith. The man who had humiliated Laura for years. And then I let him go. I shall never know with certainty whether or not I could have made a superhuman effort and saved him. So who am I to judge Grace Iles?"

"Accidental death!" the Inspector murmured.

"There's no tribunal I could submit my case to. No tribunal before which I would willingly bring Grace. I'm on my way now to see Laura. I shall tell her, just as I've told you, and I shall abide by what she says. Can you suggest anything better?"

Smith shook his head. "No. I can only wish you well."

Far across the fields, he could see Bargehouse Mill against its sheltering trees. Tonight, Doyle would have his moment of triumph. Some of the important people, no doubt, would come home with him; they would eat and drink and go on their way.

But for Doyle Wantage, when he had locked the door, there would be the child upstairs, and the girl who had brought her. And far into the night they would talk of Festivals and better things to come.

Inspector Smith would go home. He would come over to see them sometimes, he would think of them often. And always, as with Ebor Maxton, he would wish them well.

THE PERENNIAL LIBRARY MYSTERY SERIES

E. C. Bentley

TRENT'S LAST CASE
"One of the three best detective stories ever written."

—Agatha Christie

TRENT'S OWN CASE
"I won't waste time saying that the plot is sound and the detection satisfying. Trent has not altered a scrap and reappears with all his old humor and charm."

—Dorothy L. Sayers

Gavin Black

A DRAGON FOR CHRISTMAS
"Potent excitement!"

—New York Herald Tribune

THE EYES AROUND ME
"I stayed up until all hours last night reading *The Eyes Around Me,* which is something I do not do very often, but I was so intrigued by the ingeniousness of Mr. Black's plotting and the witty way in which he spins his mystery. I can only say that I enjoyed the book enormously."

—F. van Wyck Mason

YOU WANT TO DIE, JOHNNY?
"Gavin Black doesn't just develop a pressure plot in suspense, he adds uninfected wit, character, charm, and sharp knowledge of the Far East to make rereading as keen as the first race-through." —Book Week

Nicholas Blake

THE BEAST MUST DIE
"It remains one more proof that in the hands of a really first-class writer the detective novel can safely challenge comparison with any other variety of fiction." —The Manchester Guardian

THE CORPSE IN THE SNOWMAN
"If there is a distinction between the novel and the detective story (which we do not admit), then this book deserves a high place in both categories." —The New York Times

THE DREADFUL HOLLOW
"Pace unhurried, characters excellent, reasoning solid."

—San Francisco Chronicle

END OF CHAPTER
". . . admirably solid . . . an adroit formal detective puzzle backed up by firm characterization and a knowing picture of London publishing."
—*The New York Times*

HEAD OF A TRAVELER
"Another grade A detective story of the right old jigsaw persuasion."
—*New York Herald Tribune Book Review*

MINUTE FOR MURDER
"An outstanding mystery novel. Mr. Blake's writing is a delight in itself."
—*The New York Times*

THE MORNING AFTER DEATH
"One of Blake's best."
—Rex Warner

A PENKNIFE IN MY HEART
"Style brilliant . . . and suspenseful."
—*San Francisco Chronicle*

THE PRIVATE WOUND
[Blake's] best novel in a dozen years . . . . An intensely penetrating study of sexual passion . . . . A powerful story of murder and its aftermath."
—Anthony Boucher, *The New York Times*

A QUESTION OF PROOF
"The characters in this story are unusually well drawn, and the suspense is well sustained."
—*The New York Times*

THE SAD VARIETY
"It is a stunner. I read it instead of eating, instead of sleeping."
—Dorothy Salisbury Davis

THOU SHELL OF DEATH
"It has all the virtues of culture, intelligence and sensibility that the most exacting connoisseur could ask of detective fiction."
—*The Times* [London] *Literary Supplement*

THE WHISPER IN THE GLOOM
"One of the most entertaining suspense-pursuit novels in many seasons."
—*The New York Times*

THE WIDOW'S CRUISE
"A stirring suspense. . . . The thrilling tale leaves nothing to be desired."
—*Springfield Republican*

Nicholas Blake (cont'd)

THE WORM OF DEATH
"It [The Worm of Death] is one of Blake's very best—and his best is
better than almost anyone's."   —Louis Untermeyer

Christianna Brand

GREEN FOR DANGER
"You have to reach for the greatest of Great Names (Christie, Carr,
Queen . . .) to find Brand's rivals in the devious subtleties of the trade."
                                                 —Anthony Boucher

Marjorie Carleton

VANISHED (*available 11/81*)
"Exceptional . . . a minor triumph."
—Jacques Barzun and Wendell Hertig Taylor, *A Catalogue of Crime*

George Harmon Coxe

MURDER WITH PICTURES
"[Coxe] has hit the bull's-eye with his first shot."
                                                 —*The New York Times*

Edmund Crispin

BURIED FOR PLEASURE
"Absolute and unalloyed delight."
                                —Anthony Boucher, *The New York Times*

D. M. Devine

MY BROTHER'S KILLER (*available 11/81*)
"A most enjoyable crime story which I enjoyed reading down to the last
moment."   —Agatha Christie

Kenneth Fearing

THE BIG CLOCK
"It will be some time before chill-hungry clients meet again so rare a
compound of irony, satire, and icy-fingered narrative. *The Big Clock* is
. . . a psychothriller you won't put down."   —*Weekly Book Review*

Andrew Garve

THE ASHES OF LODA
"Garve . . . embellishes a fine fast adventure story with a more credible picture of the U.S.S.R. than is offered in most thrillers."

—*The New York Times Book Review*

THE CUCKOO LINE AFFAIR
". . . an agreeable and ingenious piece of work." —*The New Yorker*

A HERO FOR LEANDA
"One can trust Mr. Garve to put a fresh twist to any situation, and the ending is really a lovely surprise." —*The Manchester Guardian*

MURDER THROUGH THE LOOKING GLASS
". . . refreshingly out-of-the-way and enjoyable . . . highly recommended to all comers." —*Saturday Review*

NO TEARS FOR HILDA
"It starts fine and finishes finer. I got behind on breathing watching Max get not only his man but his woman, too." —Rex Stout

THE RIDDLE OF SAMSON
"The story is an excellent one, the people are quite likable, and the writing is superior." —*Springfield Republican*

Michael Gilbert

BLOOD AND JUDGMENT
"Gilbert readers need scarcely be told that the characters all come alive at first sight, and that his surpassing talent for narration enhances any plot. . . . Don't miss." —*San Francisco Chronicle*

THE BODY OF A GIRL
"Does what a good mystery should do: open up into all kinds of ramifications, with untold menace behind the action. At the end, there is a bang-up climax, and it is a pleasure to see how skilfully Gilbert wraps everything up." —*The New York Times Book Review*

THE DANGER WITHIN
"Michael Gilbert has nicely combined some elements of the straight detective story with plenty of action, suspense, and adventure, to produce a superior thriller." —*Saturday Review*

DEATH HAS DEEP ROOTS
"Trial scenes superb; prowl along Loire vivid chase stuff; funny in right places; a fine performance throughout." —*Saturday Review*

Cyril Hare (cont'd)

WITH A BARE BODKIN
"One of the best detective stories published for a long time."
— *The Spectator*

Robert Harling

THE ENORMOUS SHADOW
"In some ways the best spy story of the modern period.... The writing is terse and vivid ... the ending full of action ... altogether first-rate."
— Jacques Barzun and Wendell Hertig Taylor, *A Catalogue of Crime*

Matthew Head

THE CABINDA AFFAIR
"An absorbing whodunit and a distinguished novel of atmosphere."
— Anthony Boucher, *The New York Times*

MURDER AT THE FLEA CLUB
"The true delight is in Head's style, its limpid ease combined with humor and an awesome precision of phrase." — *San Francisco Chronicle*

M. V. Heberden

ENGAGED TO MURDER
"Smooth plotting." — *The New York Times*

James Hilton

WAS IT MURDER?
"The story is well planned and well written."
— *The New York Times*

Elspeth Huxley

THE AFRICAN POISON MURDERS
"Obscure venom, manical mutilations, deadly bush fire, thrilling climax compose major opus.... Top-flight."
— *Saturday Review of Literature*

Francis Iles

BEFORE THE FACT
"Not many 'serious' novelists have produced character studies to compare with Iles's internally terrifying portrait of the murderer in *Before the Fact*, his masterpiece and a work truly deserving the appellation of unique and beyond price." — Howard Haycraft

Julian Symons (cont'd)

BLAND BEGINNING
"Mr. Symons displays a deft storytelling skill, a quiet and literate wit, a nice feeling for character, and detective ingenuity of a high order."
—Anthony Boucher, *The New York Times*

BOGUE'S FORTUNE
"There's a touch of the old sardonic humour, and more than a touch of style."
—*The Spectator*

THE BROKEN PENNY
"The most exciting, astonishing and believable spy story to appear in years.
—Anthony Boucher, *The New York Times Book Review*

THE COLOR OF MURDER
"A singularly unostentatious and memorably brilliant detective story."
—*New York Herald Tribune Book Review*

THE 31ST OF FEBRUARY
"Nobody has painted a more gruesome picture of the advertising business since Dorothy Sayers wrote 'Murder Must Advertise', and very few people have written a more entertaining or dramatic mystery story."
—*The New Yorker*

Dorothy Stockbridge Tillet
(John Stephen Strange)

THE MAN WHO KILLED FORTESCUE
"Better than average."
—*Saturday Review of Literature*

Simon Troy

SWIFT TO ITS CLOSE
"A nicely literate British mystery . . . the atmosphere and the plot are exceptionally well wrought, the dialogue excellent."
—*Best Sellers*

Henry Wade

A DYING FALL
"One of those expert British suspense jobs . . . it crackles with undercurrents of blackmail, violent passion and murder. Topnotch in its class."
—*Time*

THE HANGING CAPTAIN
"This is a detective story for connoisseurs, for those who value clear thinking and good writing above mere ingenuity and easy thrills."
—*Times Literary Supplement*

Hillary Waugh

LAST SEEN WEARING . . .
"A brilliant tour de force."
—Julian Symons

THE MISSING MAN
"The quiet detailed police work of Chief Fred C. Fellows, Stockford, Conn., is at its best in *The Missing Man* . . . one of the Chief's toughest cases and one of the best handled."
—Anthony Boucher, *The New York Times Book Review*

Henry Kitchell Webster

WHO IS THE NEXT?
"A double murder, private-plane piloting, a neat impersonation, and a delicate courtship are adroitly combined by a writer who knows how to use the language." —Jacques Barzun and Wendell Hertig Taylor

Anna Mary Wells

MURDERER'S CHOICE
"Good writing, ample action, and excellent character work."
—*Saturday Review of Literature*

A TALENT FOR MURDER
"The discovery of the villain is a decided shock."
—*Books*

Edward Young

THE FIFTH PASSENGER
"Clever and adroit . . . excellent thriller"
—*Library Journal*

If you enjoyed this book you'll want to know about THE PERENNIAL LIBRARY MYSTERY SERIES

Nicholas Blake

Gavin Black

☐	P 473	A DRAGON FOR CHRISTMAS	$1.95
☐	P 485	THE EYES AROUND ME	$1.95
☐	P 472	YOU WANT TO DIE, JOHNNY?	$1.95

Christianna Brand

| ☐ | P 551 | GREEN FOR DANGER | $2.50 |

Marjorie Carleton

| ☐ | P 559 | VANISHED (available 11/81) | $2.50 |

George Harmon Coxe

| ☐ | P 527 | MURDER WITH PICTURES | $2.25 |

Edmund Crispin

| ☐ | P 506 | BURIED FOR PLEASURE | $1.95 |

D. M. Devine

| ☐ | P 558 | MY BROTHER'S KILLER (available 11/81) | $2.50 |

Kenneth Fearing

| ☐ | P 500 | THE BIG CLOCK | $1.95 |

Buy them at your local bookstore or use this coupon for ordering:

HARPER & ROW, Mail Order Dept. #PMS, 10 East 53rd St., New York, N.Y. 10022.

Please send me the books I have checked above. I am enclosing $ _____ which includes a postage and handling charge of $1.00 for the first book and 25¢ for each additional book. Send check or money order. No cash or C.O.D.'s please.

Name _____

Address _____

City _____ State _____ Zip _____

Please allow 4 weeks for delivery. USA and Canada only. This offer expires 8/1/82. Please add applicable sales tax.

Andrew Garve

☐ P 430 THE ASHES OF LODA $1.50
☐ P 451 THE CUCKOO LINE AFFAIR $1.95
☐ P 429 A HERO FOR LEANDA $1.50
☐ P 449 MURDER THROUGH THE LOOKING
         GLASS $1.95
☐ P 441 NO TEARS FOR HILDA $1.95
☐ P 450 THE RIDDLE OF SAMSON $1.95

Michael Gilbert

☐ P 446 BLOOD AND JUDGMENT $1.95
☐ P 459 THE BODY OF A GIRL $1.95
☐ P 448 THE DANGER WITHIN $1.95
☐ P 447 DEATH HAS DEEP ROOTS $1.95
☐ P 458 FEAR TO TREAD $1.95

C. W. Grafton

☐ P 519 BEYOND A REASONABLE DOUBT $1.95

Edward Grierson

☐ P 528 THE SECOND MAN $2.25

Buy them at your local bookstore or use this coupon for ordering:

HARPER & ROW, Mail Order Dept. #PMS, 10 East 53rd St., New York, N.Y. 10022.
Please send me the books I have checked above. I am enclosing $ _____ which includes a postage and handling charge of $1.00 for the first book and 25¢ for each additional book. Send check or money order. No cash or C.O.D.'s please.

Name _____

Address _____

City _____ State _____ Zip _____
Please allow 4 weeks for delivery. USA and Canada only. This offer expires 8/1/82. Please add applicable sales tax.

Cyril Hare

☐	P 555	DEATH IS NO SPORTSMAN *(available 12/81)*	$2.50
☐	P 556	DEATH WALKS THE WOODS *(available 12/81)*	$2.50
☐	P 455	AN ENGLISH MURDER	$1.95
☐	P 522	TRAGEDY AT LAW	$2.25
☐	P 514	UNTIMELY DEATH	$2.25
☐	P 523	WITH A BARE BODKIN	$2.25

Robert Harling

☐	P 545	THE ENORMOUS SHADOW	$2.25

Matthew Head

☐	P 541	THE CABINDA AFFAIR	$2.25
☐	P 542	MURDER AT THE FLEA CLUB	$2.25

M. V. Heberden

☐	P 533	ENGAGED TO MURDER	$2.25

James Hilton

☐	P 501	WAS IT MURDER?	$1.95

Elspeth Huxley

☐	P 540	THE AFRICAN POISON MURDERS	$2.25

Buy them at your local bookstore or use this coupon for ordering:

HARPER & ROW, Mail Order Dept. #PMS, 10 East 53rd St., New York, N.Y. 10022.
Please send me the books I have checked above. I am enclosing $ _____ which includes a postage and handling charge of $1.00 for the first book and 25¢ for each additional book. Send check or money order. No cash or C.O.D.'s please.

Name _____

Address _____

City _____ State _____ Zip _____
Please allow 4 weeks for delivery. USA and Canada only. This offer expires 8/1/82. Please add applicable sales tax.

Francis Iles

☐ P 517   BEFORE THE FACT $1.95
☐ P 532   MALICE AFORETHOUGHT $1.95

Lange Lewis

☐ P 518   THE BIRTHDAY MURDER $1.95

Arthur Maling

☐ P 482   LUCKY DEVIL $1.95
☐ P 483   RIPOFF $1.95
☐ P 484   SCHROEDER'S GAME $1.95

Austin Ripley

☐ P 387   MINUTE MYSTERIES $1.95

Thomas Sterling

☐ P 529   THE EVIL OF THE DAY $2.25

Julian Symons

☐ P 468   THE BELTING INHERITANCE $1.95
☐ P 469   BLAND BEGINNING $1.95
☐ P 481   BOGUE'S FORTUNE $1.95
☐ P 480   THE BROKEN PENNY $1.95
☐ P 461   THE COLOR OF MURDER $1.95
☐ P 460   THE 31ST OF FEBRUARY $1.95

Buy them at your local bookstore or use this coupon for ordering:

Dorothy Stockbridge Tillet
(John Stephen Strange)

☐ P 536   THE MAN WHO KILLED FORTESCUE $2.25

Simon Troy

☐ P 546   SWIFT TO ITS CLOSE $2.50

Henry Wade

☐ P 543   A DYING FALL $2.25
☐ P 548   THE HANGING CAPTAIN $2.25

Hillary Waugh

☐ P 552   LAST SEEN WEARING . . . $2.50
☐ P 553   THE MISSING MAN $2.50

Henry Kitchell Webster

☐ P 539   WHO IS THE NEXT? $2.25

Anna Mary Wells

☐ P 534   MURDERER'S CHOICE $2.25
☐ P 535   A TALENT FOR MURDER $2.25

Edward Young

☐ P 544   THE FIFTH PASSENGER $2.25

Buy them at your local bookstore or use this coupon for ordering:

HARPER & ROW, Mail Order Dept. #PMS, 10 East 53rd St., New York, N.Y. 10022.
Please send me the books I have checked above. I am enclosing $ _____ which includes a postage and handling charge of $1.00 for the first book and 25¢ for each additional book. Send check or money order. No cash or C.O.D.'s please.

Name _____

Address _____

City _____ State _____ Zip _____
Please allow 4 weeks for delivery. USA and Canada only. This offer expires 8/1/82. Please add applicable sales tax.